TEMPTING THE SCOUNDREL

TRACY SUMNER

ALSO BY TRACY SUMNER

PROLOGUE

An evening when young love is in the air...
Tavistock House, Mayfair
July 1808

The girl captivated him from first sight, fascination a
delightful little shiver along his skin.

As she had every night he'd been in residence, she huddled in
the veranda's dark corner, book in hand, an oil lamp illuminating
the page she brought close to the tarnished glass globe. A housemaid, she read in secret. And hungrily.

He could feel her determination, her daring, from his perch
one story above.

Determination matching his own.

Christian Bainbridge braced his hands on the ledge of his
bedchamber window and leaned into a spill of moonlight,
releasing a half-laugh at his foolishness. There was nothing
poetic about this night, this house, or his circumstances. The
air reeked of coal smoke and charred meat, rotting vegeta-

bles and the Thames, familiar even in its wretchedness. Cousin to the Earl of Tavistock, whose home Christian currently occupied, he was stuck in the slender crack between the aristocracy and the middling classes, welcome in neither.

The loneliest place to wedge oneself, he'd come to find.

After the recent death of his beloved brother, Christian was alone in the world except for the earl, a man rumored—and, regrettably, the rumors were true—to have several significant deficits of character.

To Christian's mind, the worst being that he failed to maintain his timepieces.

Christian glanced back to the pocket watch parts spread across the desk, candlelight dancing over metal coils, serrated wheels, the blunt edge of a screwdriver. You could tell much about a person from the way they tended their treasures.

The earl tended his poorly.

Tavistock had little care for his belongings, his tenants, his staff, or his hapless fifteen-year-old cousin. Leading Christian to make the rash decision to accept an apprenticeship he'd been offered with a prominent watchmaker in Cambridge. He had another term at Harrow to complete, but there were no funds, not one farthing left to sustain further education. And Christian was not willing to accept additional charity from a man he'd come to loathe.

The situation was actually as it should be because Christian had never been interested in anything but the art of repairing timepieces.

And when he was ready, designing his own.

Before this girl, only gears and coils and springs had captured his attention.

He'd asked a groom, a footman, and finally, the housekeeper for her name, because he'd felt he must learn it before leaving the estate at dawn. Raine Mowbray, he'd been told.

A young woman who now held a unique position in his universe.

Love at first sight did that to a boy.

There was something elemental about his reaction to Raine, more extraordinary than mere appreciation for her loveliness. Lust, he supposed, but it felt like more. He had little experience with women, so he couldn't accurately categorize his response.

He'd only seen her once up close, no words exchanged, no eye contact made, as she rushed through the walled garden and into the kitchens, the aroma of roses overpowering until the subtle scent of lemon and lavender clinging to her skin swept in and knocked all else aside. Blew every thought from his mind and left him stranded, like a withered leaf dangling from a limb.

It sounded melodramatic, but his heart had raced inside with her.

While she hadn't paused or blinked or seemed to notice him at all.

Which was a good thing. Christian was leaving, he was destitute, lacking in funds, family, or friends. Too young to matter, too old to indulge. His future, which was going to be bloody *brilliant* he pledged to himself right there in the cloying twilight, lay in Cambridge, not London.

He was going to make his way on his own, his awful cousin be damned.

The girl on the veranda moved the book into the light, turned a page with a delicate shift of her wrist, smiled softly at a twist in the story. He wished with everything in him that they'd been able to talk, he and Raine Mowbray. Even once. For a moment. About anything. Her voice was a mystery to him, and for that, he was genuinely sorrowful, because she looked as lonely as he felt.

Willing himself to turn away, Christian returned to his cousin's watch and his promise to restore the neglected timepiece before he left London. When repaired, it would provide an accurate accounting for a man who didn't deserve precision.

But such was life.

Christian placed the loupe against his eye and plunged into his task.

Preparing to walk away from one fascination and toward another.

CHAPTER 1

A morning long after love had been forsaken...
Hartland Abbey, Yorkshire
June 1818

*R*aine stared out the duchess's drawing room window, the oilcloth in her hand forgotten. Her intention to dust the sashes and neat white frame forgotten.

There was something unusual about the tall, strikingly handsome man who'd arrived at the estate and now stood on the crushed-stone drive talking with Lord Jonathan, the Duke of Devon's eldest son. She gave the baseboard a punishing buff, searching her memory.

He seemed *familiar*, which was absurd.

Raine cataloged his features, trying to solve the puzzle. Square jaw, dark, disheveled hair, tastefully elegant suit of clothing, polished Hessians glinting in the sunlight. A curl of amusement about his lips, lines of delight streaking from his eyes, he looked rather like a man who held a secret close. A hint of mischievousness beneath an almost bookish air. Spellbound, she watched him gesture to a passing footman who'd unloaded a bevy of cases from a landau and was struggling to carry them inside the house, the man's regard for his belongings—which didn't look like the customary sartorial fripperies the *ton* dragged to Yorkshire—possessive and intense. Whatever was in those gleaming wooden cases mattered to their visitor. His gaze followed the boxes up the marble stairs and into the house with the longing one usually reserved for a paramour.

"They say he refused a knighthood."

Raine flinched, the oilcloth dropping from her hand to the Aubusson carpet. Ellen Bruce, one of the other housemaids, giggled and winked. In the duke's employ since she was a child, Ellen knew everyone and *heard* everything, while Raine had only been on the estate for six paltry months.

Therefore she knew almost nothing.

"A knighthood dangled before him for repairing the Prince Regent's fickle pocket watch," Ellen murmured with a sly glance cast toward the drive. "Can you imagine such a thing? Royalty be daft, Prinny especially. That's what I think, if anyone asks me, which they likely won't."

"Who are you referring to?" Raine stooped to pick up her cleaning cloth, hopefully hiding her curiosity about the intriguing stranger, inquisitiveness that a house servant of a magnificent house such as Hartland Abbey should not have about a guest.

"Mister Christian Bainbridge, that's who. Friendly with Lord Jonathan since his school days, he's stayed here one or two times in the past." Ellen pranced over to the grand fireplace and gave the intricate trim a passing swipe with her duster that in no way accounted for housework. She laughed, throwing a playful look over her shoulder, knowing she had a captive audience. "It's said he designs the most accurate timepieces in England, and you know the duke cannot stand to be late for any appointment. In this house, nothing but a Bainbridge will do."

Wordlessly, they watched the celebrated watchmaker stroll

past the drawing room, his footfalls echoing off marble, providing another brief look that confirmed he was as appealing inside the house as he was out of it.

"A most eligible bachelor but a duke's daughter would be reaching too high. Although he's here to court timepieces, not unmarried ladies," Ellen whispered, breathless with delight at the opportunity to impart this much gossip in one sitting. "He has more money than half the peerage what with their silly extravagances and base business sense. And so attractive, too." She turned, her duster poised like a sword, and gave it a little jab. "He'll get one look at you, and poof, be smitten! It happened with Nash in seconds flat. You could have knocked him over with a feather after meeting you that first time." She sniffed and returned to her half-hearted dusting. "As if you would dally with a groom. Poor besotted Nash. This one, however, is *no* groom, but a dangerous man. According to the broadsheets, Mister Bainbridge only cares for wenches and watches, so don't say I didn't warn you."

Raine held back a spurt of laughter and circled the room to check the water level in the many vases scattered about the charming parlor. It was no wonder the space smelled like one stood in the middle of a rose thicket. Wenches and watches, indeed. She wanted nothing *less* than to unwittingly capture another man's attention, for her life to be dictated by his whims, weakness, or unfed appetites. Even if the newly-arrived scoundrel *had* imparted a slight quiver in her knees, thankfully well hidden beneath her skirt.

For now, she wanted, *needed* hard work and solitude. And a vast library where she could read to her heart's content without being accosted.

Nothing more, nothing less.

Ellen gave the hearth another unproductive bit of consideration. "Our duke likes to rescue people, he does. Give back in reward for his good fortune. Like he did with Miss Abigail, who has a new life. A new husband! Such a lovely conclusion, don't you think? A merry bit of matchmaking if I do say so myself."

Raine paused by the escritoire desk sitting in a darkened corner. *Ah*, Miss Bruce had a motive after all. Raine would have liked to argue that she hadn't needed rescuing, but she was nothing if not practical. She could admit the truth if only to herself. If not for the Duke and Duchess of Devon, she'd still be working at Tavistock House, living under the wicked, abhorrent thumb of the earl. Shoving a bureau in front of the attic door each night to keep him out. "My eldest brother is acquainted with Thomas Kingston, the duke's footman, and he recommended me for the vacant maid's position. The earl was reducing his staff due to financial constraints. It's as simple as that."

Of course, it wasn't, but why discuss an unfortunate situation when a resolution had been so generously offered? A resolution humbly but promptly taken.

Ellen stilled with a reluctant release of breath, her gaze going molten, her tears apparent from across the room. "Whatever your story, you're safe now. This is the finest household in England. The most generous of families to serve."

Raine sighed and turned to gaze out the window, noting Mister Bainbridge's landau was still parked in the drive. *What color are his eyes*, she wondered. How did one design a watch to be the most accurate in the country?

And why had she felt as if she recognized him the moment he stepped from his carriage?

Christian unpacked his tools in the paneled study the Duke of Devon had graciously assigned to him, the niggling hint of unease he'd experienced since arriving decreasing with each treasured instrument he touched. Some items he'd purchased years ago when he'd had to decide between a new screwdriver or food for the week. Tweezers, pliers, oilers, files, calipers. A small, French wheel-cutting engine. The velvet-lined box of crystals sat at the bottom of one case. He breathed a sigh of relief; he hadn't forgotten them. Devon had mentioned a cracked face in one of his messages.

Christian wasn't used to traveling with his equipment. He rarely made home visits—but the man *was* a duke.

And *he,* Christian Bainbridge, could have been a knight, which verified the insanity said to roam the halls of Carlton House. He prayed he didn't have to visit Prinny again this year.

Gordon Pennington, his trusty partner, stumbled into the room, swearing beneath his breath, and kicking the study door shut behind him. "Did you truly need all of these? Enough gadgets to repair every device in Yorkshire. Didn't we discuss learning to work with less?" He deposited a trunk to the floor with a thump and a groan, then sent Christian a look that said, *don't say a word.*

"Some business associate you are," Christian murmured with a smile he made sure to cast away from the man who was, in reality, his best friend. His only friend.

"I'm a guard, Kit, not a business associate." With a grunt, he went to his knee, produced a knife from his waistcoat pocket, and proceeded to pick the trunk's lock.

Christian rolled his eyes. "I have the key, you know. And remember, Penny, to the *ton,* you're my valet." Although broad-shouldered, ham-fisted Penny looked like no valet Christian had ever seen.

"No need for a key. Your *valet* trained in the back alleys of Whitechapel in preparation for his duties protecting the most expensive timepieces in Christendom. And the watchmaker who created them. Thievery, lockpicking, forgery. Gordon Pennington, at your service." He snapped the knife shut and slipped it in his pocket. "I'm ill-used in this role, to put it plainly. But the pay is ample, the attire first-rate, and the danger slight. Women like the valet title, too, I've found. Makes me seem refined."

Christian laughed and situated his tools in a neat row on the duke's rather imposing mahogany desk. "I thought it a good idea after you saved me from being gutted on the docks all those years ago to repay the favor and offer you a more enviable position. Plus, weren't we both surprised to find that you're the best book-keeping in the city? Larceny certainly fostered a talent for addition and subtraction. I'd be lost without you." He shifted to remove a folio from his satchel, unwittingly releasing a hint of jasmine. A strong enough presence to brush aside the aroma of leather and bergamot currently occupying the study. Katherine liked to scent her letters, and he'd crammed one in his bag as he rushed from his Berkeley Square townhome. "By the by, did you have the necklace delivered?"

Penny snickered and collapsed into an armchair, sending his long legs into a sprawl before him. "Your typical parting gift with me as solemn messenger, you mean? Then, yes, I did. Lady Wheaton was composed but furious. Slammed the door in my face. *After* snatching your expensive settlement from my hand." He yawned and stacked one glossy boot atop the other. "Why not give them a watch when you've decided enough is enough? I'll allow you a steep discount and even have it engraved for free. Your jeweler is robbing you blind with these tokens of lost affection."

"Not going to happen," Christian said and perched his hip against the desk, the folio spilling open in his hands, Katherine Wheaton's letter peeking from behind a bent page to mock him. His watches were personal; he'd poured his whole bloody *existence* into their creation. It was like giving a part of himself away when he sold one, which he realized was ridiculous for a man of trade.

The first time he'd taken a watch apart and put it back together had been the only time, aside from the girl on the veranda who'd knocked the breath from him years ago at Tavistock House, when his heart had wholly ruled his mind.

When he fell in love, *if* he ever fell in love, his wife would wear one of his watches. Which would mean more to him than any ring ever could. He would wait to find the woman who would understand that. Who would know without him having to tell her.

He slammed the folio shut, feeling the sting of dissatisfaction.

That was not happening as he'd given up on love.

At the moment, his loneliness was palpable but hidden, thriving despite the adoring mistresses he surrounded himself with. He'd tried, repeatedly, but there seemed little point in searching for what was not *there*. Had only been there that one time, a spark he'd extinguished by leaving before he even spoke to the girl.

"You're getting that sullen look again," Penny murmured from the chair, his lids low, close to sleep if Christian had his guess. "And we have no women, not yet, to lift you from your melancholy."

Christian shook himself from his stupor, slipped a letter from the folio, and flipped it between his hands. "I'm worried about the translations, which I'd hoped to work on during my time here," he lied, tapping the envelope against his palm. "A German watchmaker I'm in contact with tried to build a detached escapement caliber, but it failed, and he sent me details on the design in the event I'd like to have a go. But German's not my area of expertise, and English not his. Parts of the missive are incomprehensible, at least to me."

"I took care of it, whatever an escapement caliber is," Penny said with another yawn. "I discussed your dilemma with Miss Miller, the housekeeper, upon our arrival. A lovely thing with the bluest eyes you've ever seen. Like the sky in the middle of summer. Delightful. But back to the problem. There's a maid, new on staff, talented with languages." He settled his linked fingers over his belly and stretched his shoulders. "Assisting the governess with those subjects or some such. Unusual skill for a housemaid, isn't it? I guess this one loves to read and taught herself several languages. Imagine, a bluestocking residing in the wilds of Yorkshire." He toed one boot off, then the other, preparing for the kind of serious slumber only Penny could fall into, anywhere, anytime. "Starting tomorrow morning, nine sharp, you have a translator. One hour per day for the duration of your stay if you need her. You're welcome in advance."

"What an amazing valet you are, Penny."

"It's a gift."

Christian dipped his finger beneath the flap of the envelope and broke the wax seal. "Does the bluestocking have a name?"

"Mowbray," Penny whispered, definitely on the edge of sleep. "Miss Mowbray."

The name danced through Christian's consciousness, sending goosebumps zinging along his skin. He forced his hand from its punishing clench on the envelope. "Her first name, do you know it?"

Penny opened one eye, a lazy blink. "Raine. Is that French? I only remember because of Miss Miller's eyes. Like rain falling from the clouds. Isn't that poetic? I may try to use that."

Christian's breath caught, the letter sliding from his grip to bounce off the toe of his Hessian. "Whose house did Miss Mowbray recently arrive from?"

Penny dropped a bent arm over his face, shrugged. "An earl's, I believe it was. A household going through a spot of trouble. A reprobate."

"Holy hell," Christian breathed, his heart kicking into a swift rhythm. There could be no one else with that name working for an earl with an appalling reputation. The coincidence was simply too much.

It was the girl he'd spent the summer watching. The summer dreaming of but never talking to. Years cursing himself for not trying, at the very least, to make her acquaintance. To be her friend when it seemed neither of them had been so lucky as to have one.

Her image, faded like it had sat too long in the sun, rotated through his mind. Hair the color of a shiny gold coin, dark eyes, shy smile. Slender and lovely and *connected* to him in a gut-sure way he couldn't explain.

Had never been able to explain.

He turned to gaze at the verdant slice of lawn outside the study's window, his chest tight, his fingertips tingling.

Tomorrow morning, he was finally going to meet the woman he'd been in love with for ten years.

CHAPTER 2

*R*aine adjusted the mobcap that never seemed to contain her unruly mass of hair, and with an anxious exhalation, blew the ruffled brim from her face. She stood before the door to the duke's study, ten minutes late for her translation session because she'd volunteered to assist Miss Miller with a chore a kitchen maid should have taken on. She'd been delaying the inevitable because she was nervous. Agitated for no good reason. Trying to squelch the adolescent butterfly-tingle in her belly. Appalling when she was far removed from—

Then he was there, the cause of her belly-tingle, opening the door, watch in hand. As if he'd been about to check the hall to see if she'd arrived. He was out of breath, dark hair tousled, cravat off-center. But not vexed as most men of her acquaintance would be by her tardiness. Instead, Christian Bainbridge, lover of wenches and watches, standing so close she could smell the delicate scent of citrus and ink drifting from his skin, had a tender, very fetching, very charming smile on his face.

And his eyes, because she'd wondered about them all night…

Oh, *heavens*, were his eyes a dazzling portrait, as blue as the delphiniums in the duchess's garden.

14

"It *is* you," he whispered beneath his breath, a statement she had no idea how to decipher. Had Miss Miller told him to expect her? Had he been expecting someone else? Had she mistaken the arranged time?

Discomfited, she smoothed her apron, the newest in her possession, and stayed from reaching to adjust her cap. The plain, somewhat dour dress assigned to the staff she could do nothing about. Although it looked better on slim figures than it did on curvaceous ones, so she could tally this benefit. When benefiting the imposing man standing before her in dark, finely-tailored clothing was absurd to contemplate.

His smile grew as she fidgeted, creating a tiny dent in his cheek. A glorious imperfection in an otherwise extremely handsome face. "Miss Mowbray, I presume," he said and gestured for her to enter the duke's study. "I can't express how delighted I am to meet you."

Oh. He seemed quite enthusiastic about the translation session. She hoped her German was on par with his needs. She gazed up into his face because he was tall enough that she had to. "Sir, I—"

"No." His expression shifted in an instant. Hardened, a flash of emotion confirming there was more to him than the bland smile and a compelling dimple. "My name is Christian," he managed, then laughed and shook his head, leaving the door properly ajar behind them. An escape route should she need one. "So easy, and yet, ten years overdue."

She entered the room, clearly missing some element of the situation. The *ton*, an exclusive group Christian Bainbridge was welcomed into, at least in part, were an eccentric lot. In her years of service, she'd grown accustomed to bizarre behavior. And become skilled at ignoring it.

On a table by the window sat a stack of books that hadn't been there when she cleaned the study yesterday. A band of sunlight waterfalled over them, glinting off the gilded script on the spines. Christian took his place behind the duke's desk as Raine moved forward like a pulley had drawn her. Brand new treasures, releasing nothing but the delicious scent of leather when she lifted one volume to her nose. No mold, no dust, no stained pages. Not yet. Her heart tripped. Books were her one indulgence, her grand passion in a life lacking any other. But they were costly and often out of reach.

As were most things she desired.

"I just finished the one on top. Austen. Two novels are included. Her last, sadly. You're welcome to it."

She streaked her finger along a groove in the cover, delighted but trying hard not to show it. "I couldn't possibly."

"Really? You couldn't possibly? Why not?"

Raine turned, a spike of impatience racing through her. A sentiment that had gotten her into trouble her entire bred-to-be-subservient-but-at-times-unable-to life. What she found was Christian Bainbridge's gaze centered on her, or more specifically, on her finger, which still lovingly caressed the spine of Jane Austen's final tome. His eyes were heated when they met hers; there was no way to hide it. She removed her hand from the book and tangled it in her apron to hold back the tremor.

The man affected her like no other.

She wondered suddenly, alarmingly, why she quite *liked* the way he made her feel. The way his attention put her on a pedestal she'd never inhabited. Made her *want* in a way she never had, skin tingling, mind whirring, heart thumping. She felt alive. Swallowing hard, her throat clicked. "I cannot because a gentleman does not loan books to a servant in a household he is visiting. It's simply not done."

Christian tugged on a length of twine surrounding a stack of envelopes he'd taken in hand, his gaze sweeping the length of her. "Who says I'm a gentleman," he whispered, his expression caught between professor and pirate.

She frowned and walked toward him, settling in the leather

armchair situated before the desk. The same chair she'd huddled in as the duke offered her a reprieve from a dreadful situation, offered her a new life. A new life she must carefully guard. "This is a ridiculous conversation. You're an esteemed guest of the Duke and Duchess of Devon, and I'm here to help you translate." She pushed a breath past her lips. *We're not on the same level, and we shouldn't converse as if we were.* "I have one hour before I'm expected upstairs. Can we begin?"

"Of course, my apologies for any transgression. But know this." He dropped his eyes, slid a letter free from the envelope, and ironed his palm across the sheet. "I'm the youngest son of a vicar who used God's word most brutally. I was lucky enough to find my talent at an early age, a profitable talent, admittedly, and thank God for it because there was nothing else for me. I, too, have worked for everything I have; I've been given nothing. If you and I are going to spend time together, I simply wanted you to understand we're not so far apart." He sighed, his gaze touching hers before roaming to the window and that enticing stack of books. "As recompense for assisting with the translations, I thought it proper if you took the book. Any of them," he added, dragging his hand through his hair, leaving it in charming spikes atop his head.

His distress, and his generosity, sent a jolt through her. Not many kind men populated her world. She drew a breath that smelled faintly of the duke but more of the man across from her. She knew, instantly, the difference—and which scent she preferred. "I suppose I could borrow it. The Austen. With its return, what's the harm?" Shrugging, she curled her toes inside her worn slippers, letting the way her body sang in his presence capture every sense while vowing to deny it. "I love nothing more than reading."

His head lifted, his smile blinding.

She was lost.

And vexed that he'd so easily won their first battle.

17

He was lost. Charmed, intrigued.

Relieved. To know the girl he'd been drawn to so intensely years ago was a woman worth knowing, worth loving. Worth fighting for, should the situation come to that, which it would. He wasn't afraid to act on impulse—and he *always* trusted his gut. Like the swift decision to take the apprenticeship in Cambridge that had changed his life, Christian knew what he wanted.

And he wanted Raine Mowbray.

Her finger trailed across the page, a tiny, concentrating fold centered between her brows. Her nose was pert, her cheeks lightly freckled, her jaw sharp, used to being stubbornly set, he'd bet. Her hair, as golden as the butter he'd spread on his breakfast scone, fleeing the silly domestic's headpiece he'd love to yank from her head. She was slender. Delicate. As poised as any lady roaming any ballroom he'd ever been invited into. Whip-smart, when intelligent females who *admitted* being intelligent, were a rare commodity.

And, *ah*, was she beautiful.

She nibbled on her thumbnail and hummed beneath her breath, scribbling translations on a sheet of foolscap. Christian held back a groan—and the urge to tip her chin high and pour his frustration into a fiery kiss. His body was pulsing with the fantasy, every *inch* of it.

"Am I interrupting your work?" she asked without looking up, a subtle smile tilting the corners of her mouth.

He wasn't sure what he'd done to bring about amusement, but he'd go with it. They only had ten minutes left together, and Christian wanted Raine's conversation more than he wanted details on how to build a detached escapement caliber. And that was a first. "I'm sorry, I got distracted. Devon's watch repair may require a part I neglected to bring."

Her long lashes lifted, revealing eyes he'd thought were

brown but had turned out to be an enchanting shade of hazel. She hesitated before asking, "Did you truly turn down a knighthood?"

He opened his mouth, closed it. Ran his tongue over his teeth while searching for what he wanted to tell her. The truth was probably best. In any case, his cheeks flushed, saying it before he could.

"Heavens above, you did. You turned down a knighthood!"

The Prince Regent is cracked, Christian wanted to say. The watch in question was a piece of Austrian junk, not worth the expense or the bother. Annoyance, and a ragged little thread of panic, almost drove out the pulse of desire controlling him. Raine would never find him suitable if she believed a meaningless knighthood stood between them. "It was a lark," was all he came up with.

She tapped her quill pen against the desk, considering. "Did Prinny think the proposal a lark?"

He placed his tweezers on the desk, removed the loupe from its nestle against his eye. "What else have the chattering ninnies been saying?" Gossip had followed him his entire life because he presented such an intriguing subject, stuck as he was in that graceless spot between the aristocracy and everything below. A man of industry when men of industry weren't revered.

Her smile broke, spreading across her face. So exquisite, it stole his breath. "Watches and wenches," she said through her glee.

A winding wheel dropped from his fingers and rolled across the desk, coming to a stop against the duke's inkwell. "*What?*"

"All you care for, that is."

His cheeks got so hot, they stung. "My work is my passion. I treasure this"—he gestured to the tools, the watch parts, spread across the desk—"more than, well...more than any..." *More than any wench. More than I could any woman except you, I'm coming to suspect.*

But that didn't sound right *at all*. And she'd never believe him anyway.

Raine dropped her head, laughing softly. "I'm sorry. I'm being unkind. Teasing you when I should not dare to."

Christian slumped back in his chair, uncertain where she was going with this. Women seldom admitted being unkind, especially when they were being unkind. "You are?"

"I don't often get to converse in this manner." She folded her arms along the desk and rested her chin atop them, giving him a candid perusal typically only circulated inside a bedchamber. "You see, clever conversation isn't expected of a humble housemaid, isn't requested or required. Just because I'm passive by necessity doesn't mean I am in *life*." Her lids fluttered with a sigh that almost had him reaching for her, which would be a mistake. He wanted to be her friend first. Needed to be her friend first. There was a reticence about her he feared had come from the debacle that had sent her fleeing from Tavistock House.

But Christian knew one thing. If he found out his cousin, a man he hadn't talked to in ten years and barely knew, had touched Raine Mowbray against her will, he would kill him.

Calming himself, he picked up a winding wheel and flipped it between his fingers, better to have something to do with his hands than placing them on her person. "You can talk to me as I adore clever banter. I'll not require but certainly request."

Her gaze danced away from his. "I miss those conversations. I miss engaging my brain. My former employer, Countess Tavistock, let me attend lessons with her governess from the time I was in leading strings. Later, I acted as an informal tutor to her children in certain subjects. My education is lacking for a peer but advanced for a maid. Languages, reading, came easily." Lost in thought, she chewed on her bottom lip, increasing his enchantment and his physical discomfort. "I think...I'm finding it easy to talk to you, which should not be. Or rather, doesn't need to be for me to assist with your translations."

He slid his hand across the desk, unable to check the impulse. His heart had begun to thump, images of what he'd like to share with her—mind, body, soul—flooding him.

She was watching, wide-eyed but accepting, about to let him touch her.

"Kit, have I found the most unbelievable—" Penny burst into the room, took one look at the intimate scene, and bumped back against the door. "Sorry. I've interrupted."

"*Kit,*" she mouthed with a grin that lit Christian up inside. Then she flipped one of the five watches on the desk over and viewed the time. "Oh, goodness, I have to go." Making a note on the letter to mark her place, she collected her papers in a tidy pile and laid the quill pen on top. "I'll be back tomorrow. Same time. I don't think it will take me more than three days, maybe four, to translate them. There are a few words I'm not sure of, colloquial speech, but the duchess has a German-language text in her materials for the children's lessons which may help."

Christian was out of his armchair like a shot and heading to the stack of books by the window. He knew Penny was watching the scene unfurl with undisguised interest, but Christian couldn't worry about that *and* deliver Jane Austen. A bit winded from his effort, he intercepted Raine at the door. "You forgot this," he murmured and pushed the volume into her hand. She wasn't wearing gloves, and neither was he, and his thumb brushed her wrist, a desperate, exhilarating feeling flowing up his arm and into his chest. And settling. "Please," he added when he'd never begged a woman for anything in his life. "We had a deal, remember?"

Her shoulder lifted, that ridiculous cap on her head bobbing as if she was going to refuse when her fingers closed gently around the book. Then she left him standing there, the sensation of touching her bare skin engraved on his senses like his name was engraved on his watches.

Penny stepped behind him, following his gaze down the

deserted hallway, the only thing remaining Raine's teasing scent. That, and the images racing like feral dogs through his mind. Some of them lewd, he'd admit.

How soon could he make *that* reality, he wondered?

"That gorgeous creature is our bluestocking?" Penny asked in dazed incredulity. "Remind me to consider the brainy ones in the future."

"*My* bluestocking," Christian corrected.

Penny jammed his broad shoulder against the doorjamb. "So that's the way of it? Soft heart like yours, I knew it was coming at some point." He sighed, the sound genuinely mournful. "Well, now we're doomed."

Christian looked away before his face betrayed him. His severe upbringing and everything he'd had to do to succeed had beaten any sense of benevolence out of him.

He didn't have a soft heart. A generous heart.

Slightly more generous than Penny's perhaps.

But for the girl on the veranda, he was willing to expose his— even if he lost it in the process.

CHAPTER 3

C hristian was waiting for her the next morning, lounging in the doorway of the duke's study like a panther stalking his prey. Teacup in hand, he took a leisurely sip and let his gaze roam the length of her and back. His calculated study was the most erotic thing she'd ever experienced—and all without being touched. She kept her expression placid, she hoped, as her chest flushed beneath starched cotton.

My, what would being kissed by the man, which she'd spent half the night contemplating, be like if his straightforward but pointed scrutiny scorched?

Most likely, it would be a disappointment, as the two careless kisses Raine had experienced to date had been.

"Are we ready to proceed with the project?" She halted before him, amazed her voice sounded steady with such wild anticipation seizing her. A stunned breath struck as she looked into his eyes and understood she felt much more than she should have. This was dreadful, an attraction between them a breach of an elemental tenet of servitude. A domestic did not, could not, foster feelings for a guest. A guest in a *ducal* home. A man notorious enough to be written about in the gossip sheets. A man known for his profligate lifestyle and his magnificent timepieces. A man well above her station.

A man who would break her heart into a thousand pieces if she let him.

He raised a dark eyebrow and sipped from his teacup. "Are you done?" he asked and turned to move into the study.

She tilted her head in question. "Done?"

"Your face, just then, was like one of my watches when I crack open the casing. A lot of moving parts." His deep voice drew her into the room, where he added with a cunning look thrown over his shoulder, "I apprenticed with a very brilliant horologist who once told me, deliberation can arrest innovation."

She settled in the armchair before the desk, her stack of translation materials where she'd left them the day before. Christian's tools were perfectly placed, as well. A precise row, an exact arrangement from largest to smallest. Interesting. A conscientious man with the things he cared for. "Go with your gut. Is that what you were supposed to take from that charming bit of horological wisdom? For a man, I'm certain that's excellent advice. Women are not often afforded the opportunity to rise to such a challenge, Mister Bainbridge."

His burst of laugher had her glancing up from the letter she'd spread across glossy mahogany, another opportunity to dive into the blasted blue of his eyes. Another opportunity to note the wicked dimple denting his cheek. "Let's agree," he said, sliding a cup of tea across the desk when a man had never poured tea for her in her life, "that within the walls of Devon's exhaustively regal study, you're afforded every opportunity to rise to such a challenge."

She pressed her lips together to hold back a smile. "So I'm to speak freely. And this benefits you how?"

Christian popped the loupe into place against his left eye, picked up a small screwdriver, and turned his attention to the metal parts spread before him. "That, Miss Mowbray, is still to be determined."

The hour passed quickly, quietly, contentedly. There was an ease in being around Christian Bainbridge, which Raine understood was not customary or conventional. His regard warmed her, brief strikes when he stretched or took a sip of tea, that made her feel like a thick, woolen shawl had been placed about her shoulders rather than a sharp blade edged along her skin, as masculine attention usually brought. She was attractive, and men were weak. Indeed, her appearance was a drawback rather than a source of good fortune, as beauty was for a woman of highborn birth. Thinking of the times she'd had to push the scuffed bureau in front of the attic door at Tavistock House suddenly came to her, and she frowned. Placed her quill on the desk and leaned back in her chair to watch Christian work.

Five minutes at her leisure, she decided with a glance thrown at the mantel clock Christian had modified earlier, a device that had never before kept accurate time. Fascinated, she watched him adjust the wheel of a pocket watch, pause, then go in for another alteration.

"There's nothing faulty with the piece. Just a loose hairspring." One side of his mouth kicked up. "It's aging, like skin that starts to sag. Springs lose their elasticity, as it were."

"It's lovely," she murmured, unable to look away from the long, slim fingers manipulating the tool with true artistry. He was gifted. More talented than anyone she'd ever known. Foolish, to be this attracted to a man so far from her reach. To be compelled to know him better, to share the scant, uninteresting bits of her life with him.

"A Bainbridge open-face duplex chronometer, to be precise." He removed the loupe, leaving a shallow dent where it had pressed into this skin, and slid the watch across to her. "Take a look. It's a superb model. Probably the one I'm best known for."

"The most accurate," she said and grasped the watch, the metal casing warm from his touch.

He tilted his head, his lips curving in pleasure. "The chattering ninnies included that bit, did they? Sometimes gossip is as precise as my timepieces."

She rotated the watch, the silver filigree chain sliding through her fingers. "This is beautiful. I've never seen the like."

"A silversmith in France makes them. Unique to my pieces."

"Gorgeous," she murmured.

"*Yes.*"

She stared at the watch, unable to meet his gaze, wondering what he wanted from her. Her intuition told her it wasn't what most men of her acquaintance had. Or not all. There was hunger in his attention, yes, but there was also an affectionate, enveloping kindness that even his sardonic banter couldn't quell. He was a better man than he believed if she had her guess. It frightened her that she was beginning to trust him, to understand, like his timepieces, what made him tick.

"There's a spare length of chain, slightly damaged, that has no home." He nudged a length of filigree into her line of vision. "It would make an excellent bookmark."

She shook her head. "No more gifts, Mister Bainbridge."

"There've been no gifts. Miss Austen is returning to me, is she not? And the filigree has no use, consider it rubbish."

She blew out an exasperated breath. *Impossible man*, she reasoned and reached for the chain. It glimmered against her skin, a flawless fragment, not an imperfection in sight.

"Rise to the challenge in our safe space, Miss Mowbray. Tell me what's circling through your astute mind."

"I'd rather serve as a maid my whole life than be beholden to anyone," she said in a rush, the words tense, hard, shaded by a forlorn past and an uncertain future. She thrust the delicate silver across the desk. "That's what I'm thinking."

Christian cursed softly beneath his breath.

She looked up, startled to see how stunned he seemed by her words. "Sorry you asked? An honest woman isn't always welcome."

"No, God, no. I want to hear anything you wish to tell me." He scrubbed his hand over his face. The eyes that met hers were apologetic, beseeching, an indigo sea she wanted to plunge into. "I imagined it would be days before we got to this topic. You see, I'm a devotee of actions over words, and if I speak before you've had time to *see*, I'm not sure you'll believe me. I hadn't planned on this, on ever meeting you. Of course, I had things I wanted to say should it ever occur, but life never goes the way you plan, does it?"

Her heart stuttered in her chest. Could her intuition have deceived her this appallingly? Was he a devious man, after all? "You've been withholding something from me. Something I should know."

His beautiful lips parted, closed, parted again. "No, yes, partially."

"You're betrothed," she whispered and rose shakily to her feet, the notion sending a dart of grief through her. Grief she had no right to feel. No *place* to feel. How many times had she seen aristocratic men take advantage? Was she going to betray herself and fall prey as well? Over a man who had the most arresting voice she'd ever heard, the sweetest smile, the gentlest laugh? A man who was intelligent and cunning and even a little shy? A man who seemed to know her, who she seemed to know right back.

Was that what it took for her to fold? To fall?

Bracing his hands on the desk, he shoved from his chair, fury tightening his stubbled jaw. "If you think I would betray you in this manner after I've sat here for two days consuming you with my eyes, panting like a dog over a bone but holding my feelings inside for both of us, then there's no chance. I'm a scoundrel, fine, admitted, but I don't play with people's happiness nor seek to increase their challenges. When I can see you're challenged. And alone. But I'm alone, too, Raine. For years, *centuries*." He yanked a hand that trembled through his hair and exhaled sharply. "This is coming out wrong. I'm not gifted in the art of sustaining relationships. Or fostering them."

"Not according to the chattering ninnies," she returned, realizing they were arguing. Although she had no idea about what. So what if he had a mistress? A fiancée? Or one of each. It should mean nothing to her. But, *oh*, it did.

"Bringing up the gossips rags? Really? The lady doesn't fight fair."

She leaned across the desk, closing in until the gray flecks in his eyes shot into view. "You're mistaken. I'm not a lady. I'm a housemaid, and that's all I'll ever be. You're here"—she held her hand high, then lowered it—"and I'm here."

"I won't let you evade this discussion that easily. As if the tiers of society mean a damned thing to me." He grasped her hand, unfurled her clenched fist, and angrily dropped the length of chain into it. "As if they mean anything to you. I'd be very disheartened if they did."

Miss Bruce's high-pitched voice intruded, a strident call from the hallway.

Raine backed away from him, bumping into the armchair, her fingers closing around the filigree. "I have to go."

"Meet me tonight. Ten o'clock. At the stone bridge over the pond. I've been walking every night to clear my mind. It's quite lovely. And safe." He held up his hands. "I won't touch you. I'll explain everything, though I'm sure I'll muddle it up. Hopefully, I can figure out what to say between now and then."

"The truth will do nicely."

When Miss Bruce's voice again flowed between them, he sighed and gave Raine a resigned wave toward the door. "That's what we'll go with then. I only ask for tolerance in advance. Men are, you must remember, simple, foolish creatures. We often stumble along doing the best we can."

Raine strode from the study with Christian's gaze stinging her back and his delicate filigree chain marking her palm, confused and agitated, thinking somewhat crossly that she'd never met a less simple, foolish creature in her life.

Christian hadn't been lying when he told Raine he wasn't very good with women.

Success had brought them to his Berkeley Square doorstep in droves, and he knew, after diligent practice, how to satisfy. For a night, a week or two. A month. He was skilled in transitory pleasure; the mechanics of tupping weren't hard to perfect when one liked working parts and the microscopic details that accompanied them as much as he did. He was patient. Meticulous. Generous in bed, as his last mistress had shared with a level of surprise that let him know most men *weren't*. A fast pace had its time and place. As did a slow one.

He liked both and everything in between.

But he knew nothing, absolutely nothing, about quiet conversations over tea. Intimate discussions about family and politics and art while thoughts of making someone happy *out* of bed swirled through his mind. Thoughts about love filling his heart. He'd only loved two people, his brother and mother, and they were both long gone. Maybe three, if he counted Penny, which he felt he could in a brotherly, best friend fashion.

Moonlight slithered across the boundless woodlands as choppy pianoforte chords, compliments of a regrettably untalented Devon guest, flowed over him. Christian sighed and kicked at a patch of overgrown grass. Raine was late, likely not coming.

Reading Austen in her narrow bed in the servant's quarters, tucked in and away from him. Or, maybe she'd taken the book and the length of entirely serviceable silver filigree he'd gifted her on a whim and shoved them under his door, a determined rebuke. A mild breeze ripped through the pitch night, the temperature, for a Yorkshire evening, balmy and ideal. A perfect night for—

Christian halted, flipping the worn compensating balance wheel he'd replaced on one of the duke's watches from hand to hand. A perfect night for *what?*

Not an assignation.

As much as he wanted Raine beneath him on any available surface she'd agree to share, he wanted her friendship, her opinions, wishes, dreams, past, present, future, *more*. He wanted the one person in the universe he felt could ease his loneliness.

The one person he might have a chance to make happy in return. Why he imagined he could, he wasn't able to explain; he only knew it to be true.

The wheel tumbled from his hand to the grass. With a growl, he went to one knee to retrieve it. This was trouble, even if he welcomed it. Dire and unpredictable. He was in love with the woman in the duke's study, not only the girl he'd mooned over at his cousin's estate.

The sound of a branch cracking had his gaze reaching into the night, his body flooding with anticipation.

She was late. But she'd come.

Strolling across the lawn, that unflattering dress whipping her long legs, flaxen hair unbound and flowing down her back, something he'd yet to see. He clenched his hands into fists and rose unsteadily to his feet. This is how she'd look in his bed. A little untamed, a little unsure.

All *his*.

She appeared nervous when she reached him, her cheeks ashen in the creamy moonlight, her bottom lip tucked firmly between her teeth. Tugging at her threadbare shawl, she gave him a cautious smile, a tilt of her head that said, *I'm here, now what?*

He extended his hand, watched in trepidation as she glanced at the offering, caught her breath in indecision, then slowly linked her fingers with his. It was a sweetly intimate gesture, and he was unable to remember holding hands with anyone except his mother.

With a smile but no conversation, not yet, he tugged her along, over the stone bridge to a secluded spot on the other side of the stream. The plink of the pianoforte rippled through the night, the only sound aside from their hushed breaths and the distant chirp of crickets.

Penny, a romantic at heart though he'd deny it to his death, had secured the blanket and the candles. Christian had charmed the bottle of wine from the cook, Mrs. Webster, who certainly suspected he planned to use it for nefarious purposes, which for the first time, he didn't.

Raine moved ahead of him, halted, and he stumbled into her. *Bloody hell*, her body was warm, soft. He tucked his nose in her hair, his inhalation sending the scent of lavender through him.

"What's this?" she asked with a searching backward glance.

Christian gave her a gentle nudge away from his body before it provided proof of her ardent effect on him. "A moonlit picnic among friends. I'll sit on the far side of the blanket, not even the tip of my boot touching the hem of that most unflattering garment Devon has you wear. The candles add a certain sense of propriety, am I right? With those and a close-to-full moon, we're as illuminated as we'd be in the duchess's drawing room. You see, I remember my promise."

A laugh burst from her, sending her shawl fluttering to the ground. "You think two tallow candles will style this a proper situation? Mister Bainbridge, I'm astounded by your lack of prudence and your optimism that the wind won't blow them out.

Also, a gentleman never tells a woman her clothing is unflattering, even if it's the absolute truth."

He dropped to his haunches to retrieve her shawl and gestured to the candles that had defied his will and indeed remained unlit. "Go on. Please. You're ruining the most romantic undertaking of my life. And it's Christian. Not sir, not mister. I'm neither of those things, not to you."

"That's just as well," she said and wandered to his celebration beneath the stars, arranging herself on the blanket with all the grace of a queen, "because I prefer Kit."

He hummed beneath his breath, unsure what to say. His nickname on her lips sent a jagged, desirous pulse spiraling through him. Of longing. And strangely, of loneliness. No one aside from his brother and Penny had ever called him Kit. He wouldn't have allowed it if they had. The name brought too many painful memories, ones he'd sealed in a box and buried deep in his heart. This endeavor, he realized as he settled across from her, was going to test him.

Test that promise he'd so boldly made not to touch her.

Silent, he poured wine into the tumblers he'd guessed would make the trip more safely than wine glasses and handed her one. Rucking his knee high, he dropped his arm atop it and watched her tongue peek out to catch a drop of wine on the rim. His fingers clamped around the crystal as his body tightened. God, looking and not touching was *torture*.

"I wish Lady Adam's pianoforte skills were enhancing this enchanting summer evening, but alas, she's quite horrible," Raine murmured after taking an engrossed sip, as if she didn't often get to taste wine. "If she starts singing, I may have to plug my ears."

Her calm certainty about his honorable intent threw him off balance. "You're not frightened to be out here with me?"

She paused, her gaze, black in the muted light, narrowing. "Should I be?"

He took a leisurely drink, then shook his head. "No."

"You're a gentleman. A *gentle* man. Known more for your reputation than the truth. I know the difference; I've encountered the difference."

Imagining how she knew sent a jolt of anger through him. "Your beauty is tempting, but your mind even more so."

"Beauty is fleeting. And no man has ever taken the time to know my mind."

He blew out a breath, frustrated with himself. And her. "You effectively paint me in a corner when I'm not even sure it's your intention. I've never had a partner verbally joust and outman me so well. Or so easily."

That charming little dent pinged between her brows as she frowned. "What do you mean?"

"That I unhappily join the ranks of the fleeting and frail. Because I, too, find you incredibly beautiful. My captivation started when I had little notion what was in your mind, just like those toffs you describe with disdain," he admitted, forging ahead despite her obvious shock. "I only knew you had a great love of books, nestled in the corner of the veranda night after night, lamplight flooding over you as you tuned the pages. I'd never wanted anything more than I did to hear your voice. And, I suppose, yes, to touch you. My only justification is that I was a fifteen-year-old fool."

"Tavistock House," she breathed.

He nodded with a long pull of his wine, wondering if he was going to be forced to chase her over the bridge and across the lawn if she decided to run. Because he *would* chase her. To the ends of the earth. She simply didn't understand that yet—and he was just beginning to.

She placed the tumbler by her side and rose to her knees. "Who *are* you?"

"You're waiting for me to lie, aren't you? Maybe I should, but I won't. The Earl of Tavistock is my cousin, a very distant relation. Even more distant in terms of our acquaintance. After my brother died, he was the last relative I had left. I spent three weeks with him one summer before I removed myself from his household for an apprenticeship in Cambridge. I was already on my future path, already had a reputation for repairing capricious timepieces." Soothing a bout of nerves, he polished off the wine in his glass and reached for the bottle. "There was nothing for me at Tavistock House except the girl on the veranda, but I was in no position to fend for myself, to fight for more. I was a child still in many ways. Vulnerable in mind and heart from the previous months, losing my family. The earl was horrid. Belittling. Callous." He paused, the idea of his cousin touching Raine blackening his vision at the edges. "Which I fear you already know."

Her gaze lifted to roam the woodlands, the lawn, the bridge. Anywhere but on him. "That's why you seemed familiar. How you knew about the books."

"Yes."

Through moonlight the color of a tarnished coin, her gaze found his. "Why didn't you talk to me? Your bedchamber must have overlooked the veranda, and I went there every night. Mainly to escape the earl. He would come to the attic and select a maid, willing or not, it didn't matter. Not every night. Or even every week when he was in residence. You never knew, just heard his footfalls on the stairs. At that time, I was young enough, fourteen maybe, to escape his attention and my father was the head gardener, my mother his housekeeper, so—"

"I may not be able to hear this," he said between clenched teeth.

Her blinding smile, a most contrary reaction, rocked him where he sat. "Oh, no, Kit, he never..." She pressed the tumbler against her cheek as if it could cool her skin, then sighed and took another drink.

He wanted to tell her to slow down or risk becoming tipsy, but he said nothing, just sat there consumed with relief that his cousin had never gotten his filthy hands on her.

"My brother is friendly with Thomas Kingsman, the Duke of Devon's footman," she said after a charged moment of silence. "He spoke to the duke, who offered to pension me off, of sorts, from your cousin. He said my language skills were needed, his governess not equipped. Tavistock was deeply in debt, reducing his staff, so his attraction to me meant much less than the coin in his pocket and one less mouth to feed. All this delicacy, instead of my up and leaving in the middle of the night, was done so my father and mother could remain at Tavistock House until they are ready to retire, possibly with a modest cottage retained on one of his country estates. The countess is quite lovely, and my parent's positions lofty enough to make her home a fine place to live, the earl notwithstanding."

"I could kill him for making you feel like you had to run away, for making you leave your family. For making me flee to Cambridge, alone in the world with a hardened heart."

Raine stilled, placing her tumbler on the grass. Leaning on an outstretched arm, she brought her face close to his, her body moving in until Christian caught the scent of her skin, her clothing, her hair. Starch, lavender, lemons. *Raine.* Mixing with the teasing aroma of a country summer, bringing his blood to a boil. "I wish you'd talked to me. Let me know you were up there watching." She pressed her lips together, her lids lowering, teasing him, teasing them both. She had power over him, and he wondered if she was becoming courageous enough to use it.

"Don't," he warned, "not now. Not yet."

Why, she mouthed, breathless, as affected by him as he was by her.

If he had to do so little to convince her, they were both lost.

He shifted out of reach, an awkward move when he wasn't an awkward man. "Because I'm afraid kisses are all you'll give me. All you think we're suited for. And then you'll use them as proof that it's all I want."

"You engineered this"—she gestured to the wine, the moonlight—"and you're not even going to kiss me?"

"I feel caught," he said, stumbling. Then he went ahead and told her, making a fool of himself. "You know I want to. Since the first moment I saw you ten years ago when I didn't even know how to kiss! That would not have been pleasant, for you anyway."

She laughed and reached, catching his jaw, her thumb sweeping over his cheek and drawing every bit of air from his lungs. "It would have been wonderful and very sweet if you'd tried, because I didn't know how to then, either."

"Now, you do."

"Don't get cross, Kit Bainbridge. Not with your unsavory antics. I've been kissed twice. Both disappointments." She went to lower her hand, but he placed his over hers, trapping it against his cheek. "Honestly, one was acceptable. Boring but acceptable."

"I feel challenged because I've never been boring." He dipped his head, pressed a soft, searching kiss to her wrist. "I believe in accurate timepieces. Tepid summer nights and blueberry scones and first-rate Scotch. Tangled sheets and damp skin. Bottomless kisses." She made a low purring sound and leaned in, her lids fluttering. He waited until she opened her eyes before he continued, "I believe you can meet someone and *know*. I always have. The girl on the veranda is why no one has been able to touch my heart. I've been waiting for her, for *you*, my entire life."

She didn't stop him when he tunneled his hand through her hair to circle the nape of her neck. Didn't stop him when he went to his knees and fit her against him, chest to chest, hip to hip, capturing her mouth beneath his. Didn't stop him when he tilted her head, kissing her more soulfully, giving more of himself than he'd ever given. Didn't stop him when he palmed her waist and pulled her in, letting her know in graphic detail exactly what she was doing to him.

Her lips were soft, her sighs sweet, her skin moist, her body perfect. Her arms rose to circle his shoulders and bring them closer, like hot wax on parchment, a seductive, molten press.

Following timelines and building trust and maintaining control slipped away. He let his lips slide to her cheek, her jaw, a sensitive spot beneath her ear as she released a heavy breath against his neck.

Dutifully, he would record everything she liked, every little thing.

Starting now.

"You're *mine*," he whispered, his voice sounding like it had been cut with jagged glass.

And that's when she stopped him.

Rocking back off her kneeling pose, she broke his hold, landing on her bottom in the middle of the blanket.

He blinked, dazed, shaking his head as if the movement would return thought. "I'm sorry, I lost control. I don't know what happened. I swear, I only wanted to talk to you, get to know you better and admit seeing you years ago, an admission that had started to feel like a betrayal of our fledgling friendship."

She pressed her palm to her brow. "You don't have to be sorry. I wanted you to kiss me. It was everything I imagined it would be. I didn't push you away because I didn't like it. I liked it *too* much."

The hot lick of temper that had gotten him in trouble many, many times rolled through him. He wasn't practiced at accepting things he didn't want to hear. "This was a delicious taste, a glorious start. There's much more, Raine, and God do I want more, but why do I have the feeling you're going to tell me that can't happen?"

She jerked her head up, her own temper sparking. "Because it can't! There's a pleasant young man on staff. Nash. A groom with a promising future, someone who occupies *my* world, Kit, someone who has intimated—"

"Oh, no, Raine Mowbray." He grasped her wrist, giving her a

gentle shake. "If you're marrying anyone in this lifetime, it's bloody well going to be me. I claimed the right ten years ago, even if you didn't know it. Even if I didn't fully know it. The thousand dreams I've had about you since then confirm the decision, make no mistake."

Her eyes widened, her cheeks leeching color until he feared she would swoon. Then they filled with rosy-red fury. "Marriage? Should I have you admitted to Bedlam? I'm a housemaid, and you were just offered a knighthood! A union with me would be preposterous to consider when you could climb so much higher. You have patrons who would drop you and your accurate timepieces before you took your first matrimonial breath."

He settled back on his heels, releasing her as if her skin had scorched his hands. "What did you think I was doing out here with you?"

Guilt raced across her face, and he realized what she'd thought: that he was toying with her as she'd been toying with him. His chest constricted, and he closed his eyes to fend off the crimson haze. To her, he was just another feckless aristocrat when in truth, he'd never fit anywhere except his lonely crevice. A crevice it seemed he was never to crawl from.

When he'd imagined creating his own universe with her in it.

A Latin phrase he recalled from school rolled through his mind. *Contra mundum*. Against the world. He'd wanted his future to be the two of them against the world.

"Go inside, Miss Mowbray. Before I say something I'll regret. I have a lamentable disposition that's landed me in more than one brawl. Ask Penny if you need proof." He grabbed the bottle and lifted it to his lips, the taste of wine washing away the taste of *her*.

"I've hurt your feelings," she said, her voice cracking. "Kit, I would never...that is, I…"

"Mister Bainbridge, if you don't mind. Sir works, too." He sprawled to his back, his arm going over his eyes to hide whatever might lie in their depths. He wasn't accomplished at hiding his emotions, as those many scuffles Penny had rescued him from attested to. Raine witnessing his dismantling would serve no further purpose; her rejection was already stripping him bare. "Leave me to my plans to climb higher in society by means of an advantageous but loveless marriage. My plans to seduce a maid beneath a"—he shifted his arm and stared at the tree above them —"towering elm."

She muttered something he didn't catch, then said clearly, "I'll leave as you're not willing to discuss this rationally, when you know I'm right. I wish I *weren't* right, do you not know that? I'm sorry, I would never do anything to hurt you. We're becoming friends, and I've never had many of those." She sounded close to tears, and he felt close to them.

He heard her rise, shake out her skirt, hesitate, when he wanted, suddenly and desperately, to be alone. "It looks like I'm going to have a lot of time to devote to creating a detached escapement caliber, and I need you and your German, Miss Mowbray, so don't think about wheedling out of finishing the translations for me."

There. Well done. If he made her mad, she'd bolt.

Women tended to do that; he tended to make them.

She cursed beneath her breath, a most unladylike sentiment, and stalked away, the sound of her footfalls lessening until halting pianoforte notes and a chorus of bleating crickets were all that surrounded him.

He was going to finish the bottle of wine and slumber beneath the stars. Stagger into Devon's agreeable abode at dawn and sleep until supper. Let the entire household think him a mad artiste because perhaps he was. Penny could make excuses for him *and* supervise the translations, while Christian spent the rest of the week repairing the duke's timepieces in seclusion.

Then he would bolt for London himself.

Because his heart was breaking.

Raine didn't believe that love could happen instantaneously. Intuition or fate or destiny, whatever one wanted to call it.

And there was nothing he could do to *make* her believe.

Like the nick of a blade against tender skin, his dilemma was painful but uncomplicated.

For years, he'd loved someone who, when given a chance, wasn't willing to love him back.

CHAPTER 4

*R*aine huddled beneath the starched sheet in her attic bed, tugged a counterpane of higher quality than Tavistock had ever provided for his staff to her chin. Moonbeams, the same that had tumbled over Kit so generously an hour ago, poured in the small window, highlighting the dust motes drifting through the air and the despair filling her heart.

He might not talk to her again, except for his bleeding translations, a project she'd been dragging out to spend more time with him. What if he woke at dawn and decided to return to London? What if he woke at dawn and decided wenches were much less trouble than obstinate housemaids?

She sighed and touched her lips, still tingling from his kiss. Wasn't that what she'd *told* him to do? Leave her to an independent future, a footman who may or may not ask for her hand. A man she considered a friend but nothing more. A man who'd given her nothing more than a tiresome kiss.

She didn't want to live the rest of her life with tiresome kisses.

Not when there were ones powerful enough to melt copper if she only dared to accept them.

She closed her eyes and swallowed against the sting of tears. The hurt in his gaze had pierced something deep within her.

He was going to be doubly mad that she'd alerted his valet—who looked like no valet Raine had ever seen—to his possibly drunken state out there on the edge of the parklands. Where foxes and grass snakes and she wasn't sure what else roamed at night. Maybe it wasn't safe. Maybe he would get cold. The clouds had looked tempestuous like a storm might be rolling in. And...

Damn and blast. This felt like what she'd imagined falling in love would. Astonishing and distressing. Like stripping naked and diving into a calm pond. Glorious, until you looked to the shore and realized you weren't alone and everyone was watching.

Kit might love her, too. Or imagine he did. That timid girl had made an enormous impression on him. Hard to believe when she'd been so lonely and fearful. But he'd been lonely and fearful, too. Like recognized like. It made her breath catch to imagine that brilliant boy gazing down from his window above and wishing he had the courage to talk to her.

Something he'd said when he met her shimmered through her mind.

So easy, and yet, ten years overdue.

A tear rolled down her cheek, and she scrubbed it away. His odd comment now made all the sense in the world.

If she tried, she could almost picture him. She remembered a young man visiting that summer. Quality clothing covering a gangly body, one in the midst of splendid promise. Beautiful features too big for his face.

Of course, he'd grown into them, into everything, beautifully. Become a gorgeous, talented, thoughtful man. A man suited to a highborn lady, someone who would add every advantage to his life, to his business. Even in Raine's class, marriage was rarely about love and often about necessity or accessibility, property, or monies. She'd never expected love.

When Kit expected *everything*.

She snuggled deeper in the bed, her toes chilled, her skin clammy. There were a thousand reasons for her to push Kit away and only one reason not to. If she let herself love him, and someday he regretted his choice, as she assumed he would, she'd curl into a ball and die. Simply die. A marriage of convenience was one thing, but a marriage where only one person was happy...where only one person was in love...

Better to be alone than suffer such torment.

She pressed her face into her pillow, deciding to take the coward's path.

～

Christian felt the tip of a boot nudge his hip. At the third nudge, he snarled, "Leave me be, will you? I'll head back to the house with the sun. Go away."

"You're a disaster. I can't take you anywhere." Penny dropped to his haunches beside Christian and seized the empty wine bottle with a groan of dismay. "I was afraid of this. Women aren't clocks. Nothing reliable about them."

"I tried, can't you see? Romance. It didn't work."

"Perhaps the traditional approach would be better. In London better. Rides through Hyde Park, strolls along Bond Street, two scandalous waltzes in one night, done. Marriage to someone who means something but not everything. Everything is not required, Kit."

"It is for me." Christian elbowed to a wobbly sit. A gust of wind whipped in from the east, sending his hair into his eyes. A storm was brewing. He rubbed his aching chest; his argument with Raine had taken a piece of him and shattered it like china against marble. He didn't feel whole at the moment.

Penny sat next to Christian, stretching his legs out across the wrinkled blanket. "I feared this."

"Wonderful, add prophecy to your list of talents. Have your flask handy?"

Penny grimaced and yanked the dented tin from his coat pocket, thrust it toward Christian. The etched metal caught a streak of moonlight and sent it shooting across their Hessians.

Christian took a long pull, the Scotch adding weight to the wine he'd consumed in a way he knew would distress him come morning. "She's not going for it," he said with a sinking heart. Even with that scorching kiss standing between them, she hadn't considered it. Or him.

Penny's blistering gaze swept him, the judgmental cur. "Did you mention marriage?"

"I did," Christian said with another drink, "and she's out."

"Maybe we rehearse, and you can try again. You're not the best with these things. Remember what you said to Lady Lead-better about her gown? She stills get pink in the face when we see her."

"I thought she'd accidentally dressed for a costume ball, I honestly did!" He coughed and shoved the flask in Penny's direction. "Did you see that silk catastrophe? I was trying to save her from embarrassment. 'Go home and change before anyone sees you' type of thing. You dressed for the wrong event."

"What I'm hearing is that you applied your standard finesse to the proposal tonight."

"It wasn't poetic if that's what you're asking."

Penny took a drink and wiped his mouth with the back of his hand. "Ah, I've read this play before. You bumble, then Miss Mowbray says something you don't want to hear, and boom, a sulking, insolent man appears, stage left."

Christian stacked one boot atop the other and hung his head back, his gaze going to a sky that looked like it was going to unleash havoc at any moment. "A congenial groom got to her first. Someone by the name of Dash or something. Certainly the more appropriate choice. Another maid told her about that knighthood offer from cracked George, so she believes we're leagues apart. If she only knew what it was like growing up with a wastrel for a father, a revered vicar the entire household was terrified of. My upbringing was less than noble. Likely less noble than hers in many respects."

"So she declined because of societal disparity and this illustrious groom…"

"Then I got angry, and that sulking, insolent bloke you mentioned joined the party. It wasn't pretty."

"Your temper is truly your downfall." Penny polished the flask on his sleeve and slipped it in his pocket. "We're lost if we can't upstage a humble groom, however."

"It's more complicated than that." He groaned, digging his heel in the soil. His cheeks had gotten hot, always a bad sign. "Remember that girl I fancied? The one at Tavistock House?"

Penny whistled beneath his breath, tilted his head in meditation. "The paragon on the veranda. Yes, I remember, because you bring her up every time we're deep in our cups. She's mysteriously ruined every relationship you've tried to sustain, if I may be so bold as to judge. Let me guess, she's in your head along with your lovely bluestocking and you don't know—"

"She *is* my lovely bluestocking."

Christian held back a grin as shock whipped across Penny's impossible-to-alter countenance. At least he was getting *some* joy from this dreadful experience.

"Well…" Penny rummaged in his pocket for the flask, apparently deciding another chug was in order. "Consider me stunned." He issued a humorless grunt, his gaze locking with Christian's then dancing away. Penny was his best friend in the world, but discussing emotions was hard for men. God knows what tender sentiment was shining in Christian's eyes. "Almost gives me a chill along my spine. I don't believe in fate or fanciful events, or love, but damn, that's incredible. Are you sure?"

Christian nodded. He was sure.

"Then you must make her understand. All these years. She's your...she's the..."

"You're going to have to finish the translations."

Penny crawled to his feet with a curse. "I'm the best soldier-cum-manservant in England, and I'm dutiful, but I'm not crazy. And I'm *not* sitting in that stifling, regally-oppressive room with a vexed woman you inelegantly asked to marry you." He collected the edge of the blanket in his fist as raindrops began to strike the ground, yanking it from underneath Christian. "I'm scared of angry women. And tired of dealing with yours. This is your dilemma to solve, my friend." Grabbing the candles, he stuffed them under his armpits, and kicked the wine bottle in the bushes. "If you can look her in the eye and tell her you don't want her, if you mean it, then I'll pack up our gadgets and tools, and we ride back to London. If you can't, maybe your job's not done. And I don't just mean the watches. I guess I'm asking you to stop and think and not let your temper lead."

"Feels hopeless," Christian said and rose unsteadily to his feet, the rain coming down hard, soaking his clothing and sending tiny rivulets of water into his eyes.

Penny took off across the bridge, throwing over his shoulder, "That's the liquor talking." He halted on the rise, just before he dipped down on the other side, lost from sight. "And she cares. At least a little. How do you think I found you? Your lovely blue-stocking was worried about you out here in the wild, three hundred feet from a ducal manor, which I didn't point out. Came to get me. To get *you*."

Christian sank back against the bridge's pillar, his mind awhirl. Thunder rumbled in the distance, but he barely acknowledged it. It would serve him right, getting struck during a fit of masculine pique.

Raine cared about him.

She'd almost admitted that. Not wanting to hurt someone equaled caring, didn't it? Her kiss, while untutored and endearingly guileless, spoke of attraction. And curiosity. Which could lead to love. With their tempers, he expected a lifetime of senseless arguments and fierce lovemaking.

She was everything he'd dreamed of. Clever, perhaps too much so. Beautiful and serious-minded. Attentive. Kind. Unconventional in the most enchanting way. He didn't care that she hadn't been born a lady. He simply didn't *care*. He'd never wanted anyone else, not ever. Had been in love with her since the first moment he noticed her sitting beneath a dusky summer moon, even if no one—except, incredibly, Penny—believed it.

He would find a way to make her forget about that ridiculous knighthood.

About her enthusiastic groom.

He would find a way to make her choose *him*.

CHAPTER 5

*C*hristian was late for the morning's translation session.

Penny had overslept, which meant he'd overslept. There'd been no time for anything but a quick freshening up with tepid water from the washbasin and a guzzled cup of luke-warm tea. He was unshaven, cravat askew, waistcoat buttons, he noted as he looked down upon entering the duke's study, misbuttoned. He'd decided to forego his coat and had his sleeves rolled to his elbows. He wasn't going to play the part of the supposed aristocrat Raine had turned down—because his tailor *was* the best in London, and it showed in his attire—when the real Christian Bainbridge was an informal man.

He would be himself with his bluestocking and see how *that* went.

She was there, dependable to a fault, settled in the massive armchair that swallowed her petite frame, head bent, glorious hair stuffed in that horrid cap. After they crawled from bed the morning after their marriage, his second duty was going to be tossing those pathetic pieces of cotton and lace in the hearth. His first being making love to her until neither of them could see straight. He gave a mental sigh and made himself circle her to the desk. He had no reason to touch her even if his fingertips tingled with the temptation, his stomach twisting with the *need*. He'd dreamed about her most of the night, their kiss lingering on his lips like mist on the moors.

As he collapsed in the duke's chair, his fingers stumbled over his waistcoat buttons, a quick repair when there was no way to hide the shape he was in.

Raine glanced up from her folio, took him in with one of those penetrating reviews that set his skin aflame, her lips lifting in a wry smile she didn't try to conceal. With a slight shake of her head, she pushed a teacup across the desk, then returned to her work.

The tea was blessedly hot, strong, no milk, one sugar. Just as he liked it. This trivial thoughtfulness combined with the rosy tinge lighting her cheeks eased the spiral of tension in his belly. She wasn't unaffected by him *or* his graceless proposal.

It was a start.

He popped his loupe in place, collected his tools, and dove into his work, content to be with her amidst a most companionable silence. The Duke of Devon had proven to be an excellent client over the years, his watches all coming from Christian's shop. The one he worked on now was a particular favorite, a piece Christian had relinquished with what felt like despair, the substantial blunt in his pocket not enough to ease the pain of surrendering his design. Perhaps making him an artist if not an able businessman.

Christian smoothed his finger over the etchings on the sterling silver case, the whirring wheels, the coiled hairsprings. Clicking and spinning in a flawless tempo, with maintenance able to provide the most reliable part of the duke's day for the rest of his life. His son's life. Christian's timepieces would live far beyond him, a notion which gratified whenever he imagined it.

The heat of Raine's regard hit him, and he looked up in time to see her green-gold eyes focused on his hands, the flushed streaks beneath her cheeks etched in deeper than before, her face glowing in the muted illumination flowing in the window. The sounds of an awakening house vanished as their gazes locked, the scent of tea and books and ink beaten down beneath the weight of his longing, his desire to climb across the desk and finish what they'd started the night before.

His chest constricted, his body tightening.

The quill pen slipped from her fingers to the Aubusson rug beneath her feet. She must have felt it, too.

He rose, intent on rounding the desk and convincing her in a way he suspected he easily could when the notion came to him. With a secreted smile, he settled back in his chair. His joy knew no bounds.

Because he'd stumbled across the key to unlocking Raine Mowbray's sealed heart.

Christian was used to employing stubborn persuasion—used to getting his way. Used to convoluted business negotiations, and in some instances, convoluted personal ones. He called the shots and expected to prevail while playing by his rules. Raine was used to none of this. A housemaid had limited opportunities to express an opinion. Little freedom to *choose*. Like they'd agreed at the beginning of this journey, within these four walls, he would be her friend first. Let her drive the carriage. A gift he'd guarantee no one had ever given her.

A gift he'd never given.

He flexed his fingers and held back a grin as she fidgeted as surely as if he'd trailed his lips over her skin. "Would you like to see the inner workings?" He gestured to the watch. God above, she should imagine he meant something else.

His body throbbed at the thought.

When, of course, he meant something else.

But he was willing to ride this out and show her the bloody watch.

Pushing aside the letter she was transcribing, she rested her elbows on the desk and leaned in, her simple, elegant scent skimming his senses. Soap and rosewater and the lightest hint of lemon, free of conceit or enticement, like the woman. Her eyes lifted to his, then dropped to the timepiece. "It's exquisite," she murmured and went to touch, then halted, thinking better of the impulse.

He smiled, rooted to the spot, his love for her confirmed that second if it hadn't been already. "Here." He took her hand, extended her index finger, and lightly touched the watch, letting her feel the whisper-kiss movement of the wheels against her skin. "Nickel motor barrel bridge. Winding wheel. Crown wheel. Regulator. Escapement wheel." With each item he listed, he tapped her finger gently on the part.

"This timepiece will be in the duke's possession, his family's, for centuries. He'll likely gift it to Lord Jonathan. Perhaps another to Lord William. And they will gift them to their sons. Or, one can hope, to their daughters."

Christian's heart skipped, a full second before it kicked into rhythm again. He exhaled, his hand trembling where it rested over hers. "That knowledge gives me such pleasure, such pride, that it makes it easier to let them go."

She sighed, a low, melodic echo he would hold in his memory forever when he'd once wondered so savagely what her voice sounded like. Snaking her hand from beneath his, she said, "You're possessive."

He knew they weren't talking about his watches. "I've had to fight for everything I have, and I do mean everything, Raine. I don't easily share. Or give up."

"Is that a challenge?"

He shrugged. "I don't know. Is it?"

"Stubborn," she added, humor chasing the declaration.

Taking his teacup with him, he sprawled in his armchair, his gaze locked on hers as he sipped. "Flaws aplenty."

"Kit, you're brilliant. And irritated only because I didn't tell you what you wanted to hear."

He rolled the rim of the cup along his bottom lip and felt intense satisfaction when her gaze tracked the movement. "You're the most forthright person I've ever met. It's strangely humbling. And punitive."

She laughed, such a joyous reaction he jostled his cup, spilling tea on his wrist. "I like talking to you. It's been ages, forever, I think, since I could speak my mind or anyone cared to listen. It's addictive. Like I feel when I'm close to figuring out the mystery in a book. I'm so ready to get there."

"You're killing me. You know that, right?" He blew a fast breath through his teeth, slapped his cup to the desk, and leaned in until he got close enough to see the flecks of gold swimming in her eyes. His body was alive with yearning, absolutely pulsing. "I'm happy to feed your compulsion. Any of them. Try me."

Her eyes widened, her lips parting on a spent, ragged sound that tore him up inside. "You don't know me well." She drew her hands into a prayerful fist and rested her chin atop them. "I'm headstrong. A horrible cook. An abysmal seamstress. My only talent languages, words, books. I'm independent and outspoken, a nightmare for most men. No one you would truly want to involve yourself with. I'm uninterested in parties or fashion or gossip. I'm happy with my novels. A cat would be nice. A dog even. A horse. And children." Her eyes flicked to his, then to the desk. "Someday, children."

He coughed to cover his mirth, but like smoke it slid neatly into the study, surrounding them.

"Why are you *smiling*, you beast?" she asked between bared teeth. "You know, I used to punch my brothers for teasing me like this."

"Because this diatribe is enlightening as all hell, Raine darling. You're talking yourself out of this, out of me, because you know I've already decided. I decided ten years ago. Somehow, this rambling list of excuses about why I shouldn't want you is very, very good news. In the few hours between last night and this morning, you've decided we're a 'maybe'." He snapped his fingers with a grin. "My horse has moved up in the odds."

"I haven't…that is, I am…I'm not…" With a growl of frustration, she shoved to her feet. "Oh, bother!"

He was out of his chair, catching her wrist before she could storm from the room. Walking her back against the door, he used her body to close it with a soft snap. "I'm going to say this once, then we'll sit, have tea, and finish my translations. No more teasing, no more verbal fencing. I'll not address the issue again unless you want me to." He leaned and whispered in her ear, "You're in control, Miss Mowbray, how does that feel?"

Her shoulders rose and fell on a hushed breath, her arm quivering in his hold. "You know how it feels. In a world built for men, it feels wonderful."

He braced his hand against the door, palm flat, fingers spread. He wanted to be steady—and he wanted her to listen. "I'm in love with you, Raine. My first and only love." When she went to lower her gaze, he tipped her chin high with his free hand. He'd never realized how much taller he was, how slim and delicate she was. He felt empowered and frightened by his depth of feeling. To protect, to possess. "Penny told me if I could look you in the eye and tell you I didn't want you, I was on the right path. I could leave Hartland Abbey and never look back. Well, I obviously can't do that. And I won't leave without knowing I told you everything that's in my heart and my mind. A silly misunderstanding is not going to be the reason you run from me." He smoothed his thumb over her bottom lip as she blinked, fighting, he could see, the impulse to look away. "My father was a harsh taskmaster. Cruel. My mother tried to assuage his temper, which made for a most miserable existence. Walking on broken bits of china, always. Cholera decimated our village when I was fifteen, and within two weeks, I had no one. My beloved brother, who'd hoped to go into business with me, gone. My mother, everyone, gone."

Tears sparked her eyes. "Kit, you don't have to tell me this."

"Oh, yes, I do. I absolutely do. You said we don't know each other well, so here I am. Like my tools, laid out on the duke's desk, ready for inspection." He curled his fingers into a fist against the door. "Tavistock House was a desperate destination, though I had nowhere else to go. The earl not far from my father in temperament, unfortunately, which I could no longer countenance. I knew within three days of arrival that I couldn't stay. He was wretched and...I loathed him almost as much as I feared him. I'd been offered an apprenticeship with a watchmaker, one I decided to accept without delay." Laughing, he pressed a playful kiss to her cheek. "Then, I saw you. The very night I sent the note to Cambridge announcing my plans to arrive, there you were. In that darkened corner, bathed in moonlight, pressing a book against the globe of an oil lamp. I was like a butterfly caught in a net, immediate entrapment. Visceral. Gut-deep. Final. You must believe me. I beg you to believe me when I say I knew in one second that you were the only woman for me. It sounds like something out of a fairy tale, but it was true for me."

She slipped her hand over his lips, but he simply kissed her palm, this caress not playful, bringing a needy sound from her that shocked them both.

Drawing her fingers to cup his cheek, he leaned in until his lips grazed hers. "I didn't have the courage to stumble down the marble staircase at Tavistock House and introduce myself to the girl on the veranda. So I'll do that now. Christian Emory Bainbridge, pleased to make your acquaintance. Now that that's over, will you please marry me?" Then he slanted his head, his lips covering hers, taking possession, branding her as she'd branded him on a lonely night ten years ago.

Tunneling her fingers in his hair, she gave the strands a tug, her nails gently scraping his scalp. Touched her tongue to his and shyly began an erotic dance. Stepping between her legs, fitting himself as close to her as he could while standing, he murmured an approving hum that mixed with another of those enchanting sounds she freed when she liked what he was doing.

He would enjoy learning what she desired. Needed. *Loved.* What made her heart race, her skin flush. Like his watches, he'd study her until he could disassemble the unique pieces of her to find the glorious, perfect fit.

He'd spend a lifetime making sure happiness and pleasure were never far from reach.

Predictably, the door opened as they were losing themselves in each other, sending Raine stumbling into Christian. Penny peered around the open space, one brow rising, a trick he'd perfected in his chipped mirror until he had it down, only putting in the effort because women appreciated it and invited him into their beds that much quicker.

Penny took them in with a flat smile, snorting as Raine danced away from Christian.

She straightened her sad mobcap, smoothed her dress, and tugged on her apron before throwing up her hands in mortification and slithering through the doorway without a backward glance.

Penny shoved Christian back a step when he tried to follow. "Get a grip on yourself, man. I don't know what's happening in that usually gifted brain of yours, but if you don't want to ruin her position in this household, ruin your relationship with Devon, you should let your able manservant assist with this scandalous post-encounter as you look like you've been dipped in something sticky and are not yet dry. And she looked about the same."

Christian muttered an oath and yanked his hand through his hair. "I asked her again, much better this proposal, romantic even, and then there you were, barreling in." He brought his knuckle to his mouth, winced. "Cut my lip on her tooth when she bumped into me. Your timing is impeccable, Mister Pennington, utterly impeccable."

"At your service, sire." Penny gave Christian's cravat a rectifying yank. "You didn't allow for much time between proposals. A tad desperate, isn't it?" He yawned, stretched his shoulders like he'd just woken from a nap. "You think she'll accept?"

Slapping Penny's hand away, he growled, "How should I know?"

His valet's brow rose, that odious trick again. "You couldn't tell from the kiss? My, you *are* losing your touch." He released a sardonic smile and leaned lazily against the doorjamb. "At least marriage means I won't have to deliver any more necklaces to departing mistresses. No joy in that task. Remember that crazy countess who pulled the pistol on me? Can only be thankful she had no idea how to use it." He crossed the room and collapsed in the chair Raine had recently vacated, gave the air a little sniff as if it still smelled of feminine delight. "I've had enough of enraged women to last a lifetime. For my sake, I'm hoping the bluestocking says yes."

Christian strode to the window, braced his forearm on the ledge, and let his mind sink into their kiss. They'd been entangled, the scent of her storming his mind, the touch and taste of her devastating his body. His soul. When her eyes had opened for one brief moment and caught his, he'd seen something authentic and profound shimmering in their golden depths.

Christian gazed across the duke's sloping lawn, clouds the color of pewter releasing scant light, the evergreens and hedges coated in a blustery mist. "She's going to say yes."

"Again, let's hope," Penny murmured in a drowsy voice, "after you've made a cake of yourself. *Twice.*"

"She loves me, too." *A little. I think.*

"So, it's love. Couldn't go for one of those advantageous but loveless marriages, could you? Not your style, I suppose." The grunt his valet released sounded resigned and mournful. "Well,

well, well, you've let yourself be caught, my friend. This should prove enlightening. To me, in any case. Ways I can avoid the trap."

"I want to be caught," Christian whispered too low for Penny to hear, realizing it was the sincerest statement he'd ever uttered.

He wanted, for the first time, to own and be owned. Wanted to give Raine everything she'd dreamed of while securing *his* dream.

For the girl on the veranda to finally be his.

Raine dashed down the hallway, embarrassed, overjoyed, panicked. Her body blazed like one of the kitchen's ovens, throwing off heat until she feared anyone close to her would feel it. She skidded to a halt before she entered the main hall, Mrs. Webster's smooth voice gliding from the pantry. The scent of baking bread and roasted meat joined the dusty air rolling in the open gallery windows, though when she lifted her hand to her nose, all Raine could smell on her skin was Kit. Sandalwood and the faint scent of bergamot that must be in the soap he washed his hair with. She'd had her hand tangled in the dark strands, her lips open beneath his, their legs entwined like holly circling an elm trunk.

It had been, for one electrifying moment, what she imagined lovemaking was like.

Except, they'd been standing up.

Her face flamed, turning what she knew was an unbecoming shade of pink. Dear heaven, the man could kiss, quickly finding the way to unlock her passion. And, somehow, she'd seemed to know just how to follow along, his ragged sound of pleasure the most sensual thing she'd ever heard in her life. It had been natural, touching him, body melting against his, hands clutching to bring him closer.

When it had been impossible to get closer.

I love him. I do. I love Christian Emory Bainbridge.

Now, what to do about it?

Raine was riddled with uncertainty, debating between telling the adorable man yes or hiding until he'd repaired all the duke's timepieces and retreated to London when Charlotte Webster, Lady Ann's personal maid, stepped from the pantry. Newly married to Phillip, the cook's son, Charlotte glowed like a lit candle rested inside her, her pleasant personality. She had a devilish wit that came out in only the loveliest of ways, no cuts involved, which in Raine's experience was rare.

Charlotte would understand her dilemma; her marriage to Phillip was a love-match.

"Raine, dear, you look like you've seen a ghost." Charlotte wiped her hands on the cloth she held and tilted her head in consideration. "Are you unwell?"

Raine knocked the frilled edge of her cap from her eyes, wondering if she looked like she'd been ravished. She felt like she had. "Do you have time for a walk? Through the gardens, perhaps? The flowers are in bloom and quite lovely." She tangled her hands in her apron and groaned. "I have a question. A concern. About a man. A vexing, tempting, wonderful man. I'm confused and excited and, oh, so many things!"

Charlotte's green eyes widened, and she choked back a laugh. "How could I say no when this sounds like it will be the most entertaining conversation of my day? I'd rather talk about men than new gowns. And I'm not due to assist Lady Ann and the modiste for another hour."

"Likely a very entertaining conversation," Raine muttered and turned down the main hall, heading to the servant's entrance at the rear of the house. Kit, as a guest of the duke, would use the main entrance. She used the rear. This difference in their lives was what she'd been trying to tell him, to no avail. He didn't seem to care, and she wondered if she should.

But what woman didn't want to be an asset to her husband?

She couldn't see what she had to offer when he had so much already.

The morning was a warm one for Yorkshire, the somber sky casting dappled light across the path they took over the lawn. In the distance, she could see the bridge she'd traversed last night, falling in love by the time she arrived on the other side. When they reached the gardens, Raine inhaled the scent of lilacs and hibiscus, bees and butterflies flitting around her. She didn't have a green thumb like her father, although she'd spent many a day with him in Tavistock's gardens, listening to his advice about how to make his beloved plants flourish. Usually, the thought of family brought a stinging sense of loneliness, but instead, now, she imagined Kit beside her—and felt empowered.

Charlotte crossed to a marble bench surrounded by a riot of colorful blooms, stretched her arms over her head and sighed. "I love summer. My favorite season." She patted the empty spot next to her. "Come tell me about this tempting, vexing, wonderful man. I admit I can't wait to hear the story. A certain groom has taken quite a fancy to you if gossip is accurate."

Raine settled beside Charlotte, plucked a daisy from its stem, and twirled it between her fingers. She hoped Charlotte wouldn't be irritated to learn the man she wanted to discuss wasn't Nash Cartwright. "How did you know? With Phillip? That it was love?"

Charlotte clicked her tongue against her teeth, selected her own daisy, and lifted it to her nose. "He's called me Lottie since we were little, but there was this shift, and the next time that nickname rolled from his lips, my world expanded. I felt a glow. Like I was lifted from my slippers. It suddenly occurred to me that we weren't simply friends anymore." She dusted the petals against her palm. "And there was an impressive kiss. That, too."

Raine laughed and gave her daisy a spin. "Ah, a blinding kiss. That sounds about right."

"He was funny and charming, a bit naughty. Handsome.

Frankly, he was everything. When I knew he loved me, too..."
She shrugged, a dreamy tilt curving her lips. "There was no question."

"So you can just know," Raine whispered. "In an instant."

Charlotte nodded. "Sometimes, yes, of course. However, Phillip and I took years to get around to it. We aren't a perfect example."

"It's complicated. This man I speak of"—Raine laid the flower on her apron and glanced into Charlotte's eyes, then back at her worn slippers—"he's not a servant. It won't advance his life, his career, his holdings in any of the ways another marriage, to someone more appropriate, wealthy or highborn, would. But he doesn't care about that, and I'm not sure I should care so very much."

"Does Mister Bainbridge love you? Do you love him? I think these are the questions you should ask yourself. That you should consider above any other. Not if he's listed in *Debrett's Peerage* or needs funds for his watchmaking business, which I can assure you, from what I know, he does not."

Raine's heart dropped to her knees. She swiveled on the bench, marble snagging her dress. "How did you know?"

Charlotte chewed on her lip, her smile when it broke through positively wicked. "You crossed the main hall yesterday on your way to the kitchens. You were reading a book and almost walked into a wall. Mister Bainbridge was at the front door with Lord Jonathan, and his gaze followed you until you were lost from sight. His expression..." She fanned her cheeks and trailed the daisy across them. "His expression was a study in dazzled befuddlement. He had to shake himself out of a stupor as if he'd had a sudden rush of blood to the head." She pointed her flower at Raine, shrugged a slim shoulder. "He's been here before, and certainly, there have been rumors in the scandal sheets, men will be men, but he's always seemed lonely to me. Remote, without anyone except that scamp of a valet, Mister Pennington, by his side. So, my dear Miss Mowbray, what you can offer, if he loves you, is *you*. Not funds or property or a silly title, but you. And *you* are the only you he'll ever be lucky enough to find."

Raine watched a ladybug crawl along the bench and, with a flicker of its wings, drift from sight. The anguish in Kit's voice when he spoke of having no one after his family died whispered through her mind. Even with the wenches and the watches, she suspected he *was* lonely. In a way only someone just as lonely could understand. "Will the duke be incensed if I agree to marry Mister Bainbridge and move to London? He did go to such trouble to secure my future and get me away from Tavistock House."

Charlotte giggled and threw her arm around Raine's shoulder, sending their daisies tumbling to the grass. "He's a romantic! Do you see the way he looks at the duchess when she doesn't *know* he's looking? He'll be extremely happy for you. Just think, we can have another wedding in the chapel! This is the most glorious year ever!"

Abigail Frank and Rex Ableman had gotten married in the estate's chapel just after Raine arrived at Hartland Abbey, and Charlotte and Phillip had married there one month ago.

"Are you going to say yes?" Charlotte asked. "Tell me you are. I'll help you plan, and we can have a dress made and…"

Raine smiled softly and ducked her head, Charlotte's excited chatter flowing over her, the image of taking Kit's hand in the enchanting Devon sanctuary too wonderful to imagine.

She only had to find the courage to seize her heart's desire.

It was as simple as that.

CHAPTER 6

*H*artland Abbey was tranquil, hushed, servants above and below stair asleep, duties complete. Kitchens cleaned, wicks extinguished, floors swept, beds turned, basins freshened. Raine tiptoed down the hallway, halting at Kit's bedchamber door. It had been easy, a remark about the delivery of a letter that didn't exist, to find out which room was his. She placed her hand on the walnut door as if she'd be able to feel his presence, then laughed at herself for such lovesick foolishness.

She stood there for a minute, perhaps two, the tick of a mantel clock Kit had likely recalibrated signaling the passing of time and her increasing cowardice.

"Damn and blast," Raine whispered and tapped on the door. How hard was it to tell a man you loved him? Wanted to marry him. Live the rest of your days watching him fiddle with his timepieces. Translate his ridiculously intricate chronometer designs and have his undoubtedly gorgeous children.

She pressed her hand to her quivering belly.

Very hard, indeed.

The knob squealed, and the door inched open. Raine exhaled, then caught herself, and clamped her lips shut as Christian moved into view, perching his shoulder on the doorjamb with a look of surprise, pleasure, and finally, uncertainty. She took him in from head to toe. *Heavens.* Trousers hanging low on his lean hips. No shirt, no shoes, no stockings. A dusting of hair on his chest that trailed down and into his wrinkled waistband. His body was lean but layered with muscle. A body she wanted to press into service, to warm like clay with her hands and *sculpt.* Her skin flushed, a steady, unfamiliar pulse settling between her thighs.

She'd never seen a man in such an unclothed state—but she presumed from her response that she rather liked it.

He allowed the perusal, patient, relaxed, a wry smile turning his lips, that enchanting dimple denting his cheek. "Do I pass muster?" he murmured after a charged pause, rotating the tiny screwdriver he held in his hand.

She nodded to the tool. "Do you work at all hours?"

He glanced at her bare toes peeping from the hem of her dress with a raised brow. "It's what I have, Miss Mowbray. It's what I have."

She flushed, not about to tell him she'd raced from her attic bedchamber to his door without stockings or slippers. "Are you going to send me away?" she asked because he seemed to be guarding the room.

In response, Christian trailed the pointed tip of the screwdriver from the end of her ring finger to her wrist. She sucked in a gasp, her hand flexing, her knees trembling beneath her skirt. "Are you going to marry me, Raine? Not to sound missish, but if you want this"—he nodded to the bedchamber—"you're going to have to marry me to get it. My body, mind, and soul are yours if you'll agree to take them. But I won't ruin you. I won't. And I can't share any more of myself and wonder if I'll get it back. I'm in too deep for that." He swallowed hard, his sapphire eyes darting to the floor, and she knew with such sweet simplicity that her roguish, complicated, brilliant watchmaker was as delicate of heart as she. "You fear being beholden, but what if I were to tell you I would be wholly beholden as well? What if *we* are worth more than any promise you made to yourself?" His gaze lifted, his earnestness smoothing away her fear like a plane to rough wood. "I won't own you in any way you don't own me."

Encouraged by his passionate focus, she wiggled the screwdriver from his grasp and trailed it along the line of hair on his chest, over his ribs, halting at his navel. He blew out a startled breath and whispered her name beneath it. Two could play this game, she thought. And she'd always loved games. "You've decided then?"

His muscles quivered beneath the cool metal. "In 1810, as a matter of fact."

She laughed, freely, joyously, astonished by her boldness. "What about the wenches?"

With a quick look down the thankfully deserted hallway, he grasped her wrist and dragged her into the room. "No more wenches. You, my lovely bluestocking, are more than enough for this lifetime."

Turning, she rested against the door, the taper on the bedside table throwing a golden glow over a space that held his scent so firmly she felt a quiver run through her. *Bluestocking.* How odd. How enchanting. "Kit Bainbridge, if I tell you I love you more than I imagined possible, that I don't want to be without you for another moment, that you are the most incredible man I've ever met, can I have a modest token of appreciation before the wedding? Our wedding." She pressed her lips together, holding back her smile as he absorbed her adoring confession. "A kiss, perhaps. Like the one in the study earlier today. That little thing you did, when you nibbled on my bottom lip. Heavenly."

"I think I can arrange that," he whispered and reached, tugging her mobcap from her head and dropping it to the floor. Removed one hairpin at a time until her chignon collapsed over her shoulders in a golden shroud. "Your hair is divine. Never restrain it. Beautiful things should be able to follow their own will." He filled his hand with the strands, trailing his fingers up the nape of her neck and bringing her against his hard body.

She caught his shoulders and swayed, melting into him. His skin was warm beneath her questing fingers, a smattering of hair on his chest, a mottled scar on his shoulder.

Tipping her head high, he captured her lips beneath his and circled her, once, twice, like they waltzed across a ballroom. He breathed into her mouth, used his tongue to engage and attack, unleashing her rabid hunger. Bowing into him, she threaded her arms around his neck and put every part of her lonely soul into the kiss, without hesitation or fear. Within moments, they were lost.

Obliterated, shattered.

When her hip bumped the bed, he halted, a fierce exhalation racing from his lips, his dazed eyes meeting hers. "Will that suffice? For the token of appreciation?"

Gazing at him, she searched her heart for what she wanted.

Not what society expected or what anyone would advise her to do. She searched for what *she*, Raine Mowbray, wanted. Obedience be damned, she thought. Presenting her back, she swept her hair over one shoulder, bowed her head. She could feel his moist breath against her neck as he leaned in but didn't touch. Her awareness of another human being had never been this potent, desire connecting them as if the emotion held its own lifeforce.

"Undress me, Kit," she whispered with a teasing look thrown back at him.

"Are you sure?" His pupils flared, a flood of dark black. "We have time. Thousands of nights."

She closed her eyes as the screwdriver slipped from her hand to the carpet. "I love you. And I want our life, the 'we' you spoke of, to start right now."

Goosebumps exploded along her arms as he went to work on

her practical gown fit for summer servitude and nothing more, loosening the tie at her neck, releasing the hook and eyelets at her waist. The material drooped, and Christian swept his hand around her hips, pulling her back against his aroused body as his lips fell to her neck. Teeth nipping, tongue soothing, her muffled sigh expressed her arousal, her *impatience*.

"A slim form such as yours does not need a corset," he said into the curve of her shoulder.

She turned in his arms, letting her dress puddle at her feet. "Just how well do you know women's apparel, Kit Bainbridge?"

He cupped her cheek, tilted her face up. "I can't recall anyone before you. You're all I desire. My heart, my soul. There's no one else. Really, there never has been."

He was skilled, even if she wished he wasn't, removing her frayed petticoat and chemise while kissing the very life from her, until she stood before him in a pool of spent clothing, longing forging a persuasive path from her inflamed mind to her tingling toes. When she shivered and made to cross her hands over her chest, he held her arms by her side. "Oh, no. You are breathtaking, more beautiful than I'd dreamed, and I've spent many nights dreaming, Raine. But let's level the playing field, I agree. Where you go, I follow." Stepping back, his fingers went to the fall of his breeches, unbuttoning as her heart raced. He wore no drawers, and when he flicked open the final button and kicked aside the garment, there wasn't a stitch of cotton or linen between them.

She hadn't known what to imagine, but *he* was the beautiful one. Lithe and lean, his skin golden, a body in ideal balance. Her gaze traveled below his waist. A prolonged breath escaped through her teeth as he took himself in hand and stroked, slowly, his eyes locked on hers.

"Are you certain you'll fit?"

"Trust me, love, we were made for each other." Smiling, he gave her a gentle push that sent her across the feather mattress, where he then flooded over her. His serene patience evaporated the moment his skin met hers, his hands roaming as his lips reclaimed.

It was an assault, sure, steady, relentless.

Hunger, reckless passion.

Desperation.

With a hoarse murmur, she gripped his hip, his shoulder, nails scraping his back, hardly knowing how she'd come to be squeezed into this molten, quivering mass of flesh, not one whit of intent beyond a maddening race for pleasure. His hand cupped her breast, thumb sweeping her nipple, circling, and sweeping again. Her back arched off the mattress, and she let out a frayed sound, interrupting a kiss she could no longer sustain.

"Duly noted," he murmured and tugged the peaked nub between his lips, biting lightly until she felt the hard pinch in her fingertips, the soles of her feet, the backs of her knees. Her rough moan shattered the stillness, her hands falling from him to twist in the counterpane, her body curving into his touch. A sharp gust ripped in the open window and swept her, cooling skin reheated moments later. Stunned, she lay there as he kissed one breast and palmed the other, switched, then switched again, until she could absorb nothing but their gulping, ragged breaths, walled inside a house of pleasure.

"Your heartbeat is racing beneath my lips. I'm crazy for the feel of you." He shifted his hips with a groan, his cock settling against her warm folds, a natural, flawless fit. They moved together, creating a rhythm he echoed with his tongue when he captured her mouth beneath his.

Awash in sensation, her fingers rose to tangle in his hair as she begged for more.

He snaked his hand between their bodies, palming her thigh, delving between her legs. He queried lightly, gently, sliding a finger inside her, a leisurely effort that left her trembling, strung tight, expectant. *Wanting.* This was *nothing* like what she'd done to herself on those solitary nights in her bed, her knowledge of her body slight but her yearning fierce.

It was as if he knew her better than she knew herself.

Knew exactly where to touch her, *how* to touch her.

"There. More, oh, Kit," she whispered against his shoulder as he inserted another finger, biting his skin to emphasize her plea. *"There."*

When she went to touch him, feel his rigid length for the first time, he lifted her arm high over her head, stretching her body out like one of his chains beneath him. "My bluestocking arrives, wild and greedy. I would love to have your hands on me, but if that happens now, I'll come in seconds." Rising over her, he braced his weight on his forearm, never releasing his hold on her, below the waist or above. "Look at me, love."

When she did, she found his gaze stunned, brow moist, cheeks glowing, lips parted—truthfully looking as devastated as she felt. "What?" she murmured, lost, trying to catch what she'd missed. "Why did you stop?"

He grinned, laughed softly, looking so boyishly handsome her heart stuttered. "I love you, Raine, with everything inside me, and I'll thank God every day for sending you to me again. I just wanted you to know before I took you." Astonishing admission released to the night, he positioned his body and slid inside her, just enough. Not nearly enough. The feeling of fullness was astounding, frightening...magnificent.

He caught her thigh, angling her leg over his hip and stroked, taking calm possession until they were locked, hip to hip. Tunneling his arm beneath her, he set a fundamental rhythm, a cadence neither reckless nor rushed. An elegant tempo of slick skin, seeking hands, broken, uneven kisses. Half-breaths and fractured moans. She answered his earnest questions—*is this okay, does it hurt*—his aroused murmurs a bottomless tremor in her ear. And he followed her instructions—*faster, deeper, there*—with almost perfect devotion.

She moved against him, drove him, drove herself, with confidence born of instinct.

Any pain was fleeting, minor, and after a few moments, nonexistent. The world constricted to his frantic directions, his clutching hold, his weight, the salty taste of his skin. The tart scent of them riding the air, the sheets, their bodies.

She tried to tell him what was happening inside her, the creeping sensation of being swept away on a roaring tide, but the tremors racking her made speech challenging and rational thought impossible. But he understood, reaching between them, a final, prolonged touch between her legs all it took to unleash her climax. An endless release that drew reason and breath from her until she was boneless, floating on a sea of twisted silk bedding, helpless to do anything but allow passion to take her.

His answering groan and thrust deep, deep inside her confirmed he'd reached this wondrous place, too.

They gasped and clung, lips touching, chests heaving, brow to brow, cheek to cheek. He tried to say something but finally shook his head and collapsed to his side, bringing her with him. Wordlessly, he tucked her against his body. She opened her mouth, feeling she must say *something*, but he shook his head again and whisked his finger across her lips. *Not yet.*

Before she could take another breath, her solicitous, remarkable intended tumbled into an exhausted sleep.

She could only sigh, laugh, and join him, her heart lighter than a butterfly's wings.

She wasn't alone.

The panicked realization ripped through Raine's mind before she remembered. Blinking, she rose to her elbow, her hair a flaxen shroud falling over the man whose shoulder she'd been using as a pillow. Christian's breathing was even, his lids fluttering with dreams she hoped she inhabited. She looked to the window, determined it to be an hour or so before dawn. She'd need to leave him soon, creep back to the attic, and pretend she'd been there all night.

Instead of what she'd been doing, which was planning her future.

Raine dropped her cheek to her hand, allowing herself a moment to watch him. Record every inch of him as she'd been too occupied during the night to do. The sheet was tangled about his long legs and drawn judiciously to his trim waist. His belly rose and fell with his breaths. She trailed a finger up his chest, traced a crescent scar on his neck, marveled at eyelashes that looked like the tips had been dipped in amber.

He wasn't perfect. He had a temper. He was impulsive. Even a little arrogant. But he was also generous. Considerate. Shy, unbelievably. And so talented he made her proud when she'd no reason to claim the sentiment.

He was a sincere man in a society of impersonators.

And he was *hers*.

"Your scrutiny is lighting me up like you pressed a glowing ember against my skin," he whispered and rolled over her, their bodies settling flawlessly into place. "I'm a watchmaker without a timepiece. How long do we have?" He gazed to the window, chewed his bottom lip in deliberation. "I have an appointment with Devon at nine, the courtesy of informing him of our upcoming nuptials before any bit of nonsense about us is repeated. In light of your father not being here for me to ask. Though once we return to London, it's my first task."

Her heart squeezed. Love was a powerful drug, indeed. "We have ten minutes, maybe fifteen."

He nodded, the keen glow in his eyes sending a serrated pulse through her. "I'll make it work."

"We'll see," she said as he dipped his head to nibble on a sensitive spot beneath her jaw. Both times during the night had taken longer, *much* longer.

"Oh, love, just watch me." His hand swept low, his fingers, his tongue, his teeth following just behind, turning her world upside down. "And you know what they say. Third time's a charm."

So, she did. And it was.

CHAPTER 7

*C*hristian was rarely nervous.

However, the Duke of Devon's regard across the breakfast table was unflinching, rather like Christian had felt upon being summoned to the headmaster's office at Harrow. Which, due to his tenacious nature, had occurred often.

After escorting Raine to her attic chamber without incident just before dawn, he'd taken a stroll around the estate, nerves snapping, pulse drumming. Nervousness was allowed; it wasn't every day a man publicly professed his love and intention to marry the woman of his dreams. Across the sloping lawn, over the bridge, and past the spot where he and Raine had shared the first of what would surely be many arguments, he'd considered his future and his extreme good fortune.

He was, after all, gaining a passionate wife.

And passionate women didn't always do what their men wanted them to.

When the sun had risen high enough in a vivid blue sky to designate it appropriate, he'd gone in search of James Hampton, the fourth Duke of Devon. Surprisingly, Christian was directed to the breakfast room, where His Grace, an early riser unlike most of the useless fops in the *ton* according to the footman, was having tea while reviewing an ironed edition of *The Times*.

To say His Grace's glittering green gaze could cut glass as he waited for his watchmaker to get to the point would be apropos. Christian sipped his tea when he much preferred coffee and practiced his entry into the conversation. *You see, Your Grace, ten years ago…*

"Let me expedite the process as you're about to splash tea on your waistcoat. You've come to alert me to the fact that Miss Mowbray will not be in my employ for any longer than it takes you to finish calibrating my clocks. Does that adequately summarize the situation?"

Christian's cheeks stung, emotion flowing freely across his face an embarrassing predicament since he was a child. And then it occurred to him that someone in the house may have seen them sneaking through the halls this morning, fingers linked, faces aglow. "I don't… that is to say, Miss Mowbray…"

The duke laughed, bringing his napkin to his lips to hide it. "You've not been caught if that's your concern. And if it is, I'm heartily glad you're making the expedient decision to offer for the girl." He dusted his lips with the linen square and laughed again, truly the first time Christian had known the man to show such cheerfulness. Being a source of entertainment was starting to nip at his self-esteem as much as embarrassment had his cheeks. "Calm down, my man. Miss Mowbray spoke to someone in the household, a request for feminine advice, I believe. It traveled from there, quite swiftly, into my ears. I'm a fair taskmaster, Bainbridge, so my staff talks to me. I know it's unheard of in some aristocratic families, but I prefer it to surviving on a bolster of fear and intimidation."

Christian placed his cup on the saucer before he dribbled tea as the duke had predicted. "The particulars aren't valuable to anyone but us, but I've loved her for ten years. This isn't a chance occurrence for me, random temptation or some such. Happening upon her here, in your employ, is nothing short of a miracle. I'll go to any length to secure her happiness. You have my word."

A boy raced into the room and threw himself at the duke. "Father! You must come and see what I've built. It's simply marvelous. Miss Daisy said it's the best castle she's ever seen!"

Devon ruffled his son's hair and gifted him with a loving smile. "I'll come straightaway, Nicholas. Just give me a moment to finish my discussion with Mister Bainbridge."

Nicholas turned to Christian with an impish smile. "You're the watchmaker."

"I am indeed. I wasn't much older than you when I started taking timepieces apart and putting them back together." He pulled a center wheel from his waistcoat pocket and offered it to the boy. Nicholas snatched it from Christian with a gasp of delight. Christian's heart softened, thinking of a child with Raine's golden eyes someday staring up at him. "I'm working on Philip Webster's pocket watch this morning. If you come to your father's study in one hour, if your governess allows it, I'll show you exactly where it fits within the other parts. Maybe I'll even, if you have a very steady hand, let you tighten a case screw."

Nicholas traced his finger over the wheel. "I have a steady hand like no other. I'm a Devon."

Christian grinned, charmed. "Well, then, you'll be an ace at it right off."

The duke gave his son a nudge. "Back to the nursery. Tell Miss Daisy one hour, in my study, for a watchmaking lesson. Thank Mister Bainbridge for the wheel."

Nicholas bowed dutifully and offered his thanks before bolting from the room.

"You're good with children," Devon said with a speculative look in his eye.

Christian fiddled with his silverware, his gaze going to a dour landscape hanging on the wall behind the duke. "I want a family. As it is, I have none."

The duke wiped at a smudge on the table, then placed his napkin in his lap. "I can speak with Vicar Rawley if you'd like to have the ceremony here. My chapel is exceedingly lovely if I do say so myself. We've recently hosted two weddings, and it didn't take long to arrange either. Then, you can get started right away on that family you're seeking."

Christian blinked, stunned by the offer. He would have to speak to Raine, but he'd like nothing more than to secure her hand before they returned to London. "Is marriage easy?" he blurted out, having no idea this would fall from his lips.

The duke's teacup and saucer rattled as he bumped them, glee splitting his cheeks. "Who told you that balderdash? Easy? What woman have you ever found to be easy? But the easy ones, my friend, are also *boring*. You want to avoid monotony at all costs. My duchess has never bored me a day in my life."

"Oh, Raine's far from boring. Or easy, come to think of it." He frowned as he recalled their argument beside the bridge, the way he'd had to practically beg her to marry him. "Very intelligent but rather stubborn, not to place too fine a point on it." Suddenly, the way they'd challenged each other with bold, teasing touches and stimulating conversation until dawn clouded his mind and tightened his body.

"She sounds perfect. And from the smile on your face, I'd say you agree."

Christian rose and gave the duke a shallow bow. "Far from perfect, Your Grace, only perfect for me."

Then he went to find the perfectly stubborn woman who would be his wife.

EPILOGUE

A romantic morning two months later...
Berkeley Square, London

"K it," Raine said as she stumbled over a wrinkle in the carpet, "I'm going to trip. Let me see."

He laughed, a sound she would never tire of hearing, his hand shifting from where he held it over her eyes, allowing a burst of sunlight to sneak in and dust her face. His body was pressed against hers as he guided her down the hallway of their London townhouse, and she gave her bottom a little wiggle to throw him off his mark.

"Oh, no, my lovely bluestocking. You're not using that trick on me. Penny nearly walked in on us in the morning room last week, or have you forgotten? The man doesn't knock and you're insatiable. Cross purposes I'm left to safely coordinate."

"I thought you *liked* that I'm greedy where you're concerned."

Christian halted, tilted Raine's chin, and covered her lips in a heated side-kiss that left them both dazed. "Where was I headed again?" he murmured against the nape of her neck once his breath had settled.

Raine lifted her gaze to his bottomless blue one, love a rushing tide through her veins. "It's a surprise, so I don't know!"

"Ah, yes." Christian nudged her toward a paneled door at the end of the hall. "I remember now. Your touch is finally loosening its hold on me."

"But this is your new study," she said and glanced back at him. "You had the carpenters in all week. I haven't stepped inside, not once, as you requested, though I don't know what trouble I could have—"

He reached around her and opened the door.

She peeked inside, then leaned back into him with a low sigh. "Oh…*Kit.*"

"Go on." He gave her another nudge, pushing her into the room.

She looked around, turned a full circle in wonder. The space was perfect.

It was her. And *him*.

Sunlight a bold wash over furnishings in shades of blue and green, her favorite colors. A magnificent globe showing the constellations, because she and Kit liked to gaze at the sky during their walks through their lush Mayfair garden. A set of stately library chairs situated before a blazing hearth. A brocade chaise in the corner, fresh flowers in a vase on the table beside it. Kit knew she liked to read and nap, and that she loved the sweet scent of wildflowers. Floor-to-ceiling shelves housing more volumes than she could read in a lifetime seized her imagination as she walked into the room. Crossing to the mahogany book-cases, she ran her finger down a stiff leather spine and drew in the refreshing scent of new books. "You're spoiling me. New clothes and my very own phaeton. A personal account, a staff at my disposal. I'm completely ruined for life."

He closed the door to the library—*her* library—and leaned against it. "You're right, I am. And, damn, I'm enjoying it."

She turned to face him, propped her hip against the bookshelf, and willed her heart to quiet its mad romp. She searched her mind for what to say, how to thank him, how to *tell* him. But only tears came, in great, heaving gulps.

He reached her in seconds and pulled her into his arms. "Raine, don't. This is meant to be the happiest of places. Almost from the first moment at the duke's home, I've dreamed about creating this spot for you. Don't cry. Please, you'll have me on my knees in moments."

She melted into him, his heart thumping beneath her cheek. "I love it. I love *you*. But you don't have to...do so much." She sniffled, unused to emotional displays when she'd been profoundly expressive since the day of their wedding at Hartland Abbey five weeks earlier. "Give so much."

He tipped her chin high, his smile contrite. "This next bit may not help your tears subside."

"*What?*" she breathed. "There's more?"

He reached in his trouser pocket, retrieved a small wrapped parcel with a hand that shook. "I'd like to say this is nothing, but it's everything. More than the sapphire on your finger, more than this library and the phaeton put together." Tapping the package to his chest, he whispered, "This is my heart."

She unwrapped the parchment, knowing before she looked inside what he'd given her. The watch was delicately crafted, smaller, and more elegant than his usual pieces; the silver case etched with roses interwoven with her initials. The chain was one she recognized. "I thought I'd lost this," she murmured and brought the timepiece to her chest.

"Too fine to be a bookmark, I agree."

"There was never anything wrong with the filigree, was there?"

He shook his head. "No. But like my heart, I knew it was yours. There's an inscription on the inside."

Snapping the case open, she saw the words and felt her heart drop: *at first sight.* "Kit…" Her eyes stung, and she blinked rapidly. "I will treasure this forever."

He pressed a tender kiss to her brow, her temple, her cheek. "Darling, I'm a watchmaker. This can't be that much of a surprise."

"But you've never," she sniffled again and tucked herself into him, "the wenches."

His chest rumbled with his laughter. "Never have I given a wench a watch. You are the first. The only."

"That's good," she said into his now-damp linen shirt. "Because when the *ton* sees this, every woman in London will demand one. Prinny will have you make one for Maria Fitzherbert, you can certainly bet."

"I'll avoid that if I can." Taking her shoulders, he moved her back a step and reached into his trouser pocket.

"Oh, no more, Kit." She backed away, shaking her head until her hair fell like a shroud around her face. "My heart can't take it."

He grinned, a wicked, knowing turn of his lips. "This gift, the third and final for today, is perhaps more for me." Crossing to the door, he fit a key into the lock and turned the tumblers with a snap. "The sturdiest bolt in England, or so I'm told. Enough to keep out even the most inquisitive of valets."

"Penny doesn't have a copy?"

Christian pocketed the key and leaned against the door with a licentious smirk. "No, and he'll never get one. This room is *ours*."

She tilted her head toward the chaise lounge. "That looks sturdy."

"Hmm, very. I selected it myself."

Giving her watch a swift glance, she crooked her finger, beckoning. "Do you have time to assist me with a project?" She flipped a button on her bodice. "A particularly knotty one, requiring a most refined touch."

Everything he felt for her swept his face, filled his eyes—

matching every wondrous thing filling hers. Pushing off the door, he moved to her. "Darling, I thought you'd never ask."

The lock held.

And the love lasted.

THE END

A defiant society outcast.
A forbidding rogue who doesn't believe in love.
A passionate wager.

Daughter of an earl, Lady Hildegard Templeton hasn't conformed to what society expects from a woman of her station. Industrious and unique, she's created an emboldened organization for women on the cusp of marriage, The Duchess Society. Called a bluestocking to her face and worse behind closed salon doors, she vows to marry for love. And nothing but. Although the emotion has never shown itself to her. Until she meets him.

Bastard son of a viscount and king of London's sordid streets, Tobias Streeter has spent a lifetime building his empire, and he needs the Duchess Society to find a suitable wife. An asset to expand his worth in society's eyes. But he vows his search will have nothing to do with love and everything to do with vengeance. Until he meets her.

Soon, Tobias and Hildy's plans are in turmoil as they choose between expectation, passion, and love.

CHAPTER 1

Limehouse Basin, London, 1822

She'd taken this assignment on a dare.

A dare to herself.

Unbridled curiosity had driven her, the kind that killed cats. When it was just another promise-of-rain winter day. Another dismal society marriage the Duchess Society was overseeing.

Another uninspiring man to investigate.

Hildegard Templeton told herself everything was normal. The warehouse had looked perfectly ordinary from the grimy cobblestones her post-chaise deposited her on. A sign swinging fearlessly in the briny gust ripping off the Thames—*Streeter, Macauley & Company*—confirming she'd arrived at the correct location. A standard, salt-wrecked dwelling set amongst tea shops and taverns, silk merchants and ropemakers. Surrounded by shouting children, overladen carts, horses, dogs, vendors selling sweetmeats and pies, and the slap of sails against ships' masts. A chaotic but essential locality, with cargo headed all over England but landing in this grubby spit of dockyard first.

When she'd stepped inside, she halted in place, realizing her blunder in assuming anything about Tobias Streeter was *normal*.

Hildy knew nothing about architecture but knew this was not the norm for a refurbished warehouse bordering the Limehouse Basin Lock. A suspect neighborhood her post-boy hadn't been pleased to drive into—or be asked to wait *in* while she conducted her business. Honestly, the building was a marvel of iron joists, girders, and cast-iron columns with ornamental heads. With a splash of elegant color—crimson and black. What she imagined a gentleman's club might look like, a refined yet dodgy sensibility she found utterly... *charming*. And entirely unnecessary for a building housing a naval merchant's headquarters.

Her exhalation left her in a vaporous cloud, and she gazed around with a feeling she didn't like as the piquant scent of a spice she identified as Asian in origin enveloped her.

A feeling she wasn't accustomed to.

Miscalculation.

As she would admit only to her business partner, Georgiana, the newly minted Duchess of Markham: *I fear I've botched the entire project*. She'd taken society's slander as truth—shipping magnate, Romani blood, profligate bounder, and the most noteworthy moniker the *ton* had ever come up with—and made up her mind about the man, concocting a wobbly plan unsupported by proper research. A proposal built on assumptions instead of *fact*. Sloppy dealings were very unlike her. Ambition to secure the agreement to advise the Earl of Hastings's five daughters as they traveled along their matrimonial journey—the eldest currently set on marrying the profligate bounder—had risen above common sense.

Hildy took a breath scented with exotic spice and tidal mud and stepped deeper into the warehouse, locking her apprehension out of sight. She wasn't going to back down now, not when she had *five* delightful but wholly unsupervised women who would make terrific disasters of their marriages without the Duchess Society to guide them.

Marriages much like her parents' were an aberration staining her memories until she wanted none of the institution. They needed her, these girls, and she needed *them*. To prove her life wasn't a tale as ordinary as the building she'd expected to find herself in this morning—society outcast, bluestocking. Spinster. Not that it mattered what they thought of her; she'd rejected the expectations the *ton* had placed on her from the first moment.

"Looking for Streeter, are ya?"

Hildy turned in a swirl of flounces and worsted wool she wished she'd rejected for this visit when a simple day dress would have sufficed. Perhaps one borrowed from her maid.

The man who'd stumbled upon her lingering in the entrance to the warehouse was tall enough to have her arching her neck to view him from beneath her bonnet's lime silk brim. And built like one of those ships moored at the wharf outside. "Tobias Streeter, yes."

The brute gave the tawny hair lying across his brow a swipe, removed the cheroot from his lips, and extinguished it beneath the toe of his muddy boot in a gesture she didn't think the architect of this impressive building would appreciate. "He expecting ya?"

They make them rude in the East End, Hildy decided with a sigh. "Possibly." If he'd been alerted by his future father-in-law, *yes*.

"Who's calling?" he asked gruffly, digging in his pocket and coming up with another cheroot, even as the bitter aroma from the first still enveloped them. "Apologies for asking, but we don't get many of your kind round here. Some kinds"—he chuckled at his joke and swiped the tapered end of the cheroot across his bottom lip—"just not *your* kind."

Hildy shifted the folio she clutched from one gloved hand to the other. Her palms had started to perspire beneath kid leather. This man was playing with her, and she didn't like participating in games she wasn't sure she could win. "Lady Hildegard Templeton," she supplied, using the honorific when she rarely did. "Of the Duchess Society."

The impolite brute arrested his effort to remove a tinderbox from his tattered coat pocket. "The Mad Matchmaker," he whispered, his cheroot hitting the glossy planks beneath their feet. Horrified, he backed up a step as if she had a contagious disease.

A rush of blood flooded her. *Temper*, she warned herself. *Not here.* The blush lit her cheeks, and she cursed the man standing stunned before her for causing it. "That ridiculous sobriquet is not something I respond—"

"Sobriquet," a voice full of laughter and arrogance intoned from behind her. "Go back to unloading the shipment from Spain, Alton. I have this."

When she turned to face the man she assumed was Tobias Streeter, she wanted to be in control because that was how this day was going to go. Confident. Poised. Looking like a businesswoman, not a lady. Not a *matchmaker*—which she *wasn't*. She longed to tell him what she thought of the rude entry to his establishment when he hadn't known she was coming.

Instead, she felt flushed and damp, unprepared based on a split-second judgment of the glorious building she stood in. Adding to that, the niggling sense that she'd made a colossal error in calculating her opponent.

And then Hildy merely felt *thunderstruck*.

Because, as he stepped out of the shadows and into the glow cast from the garnet sconce at his side, she realized with a heavy heart that Tobias Streeter, the Rogue King of Limehouse Basin, was the most attractive man she'd ever seen.

Which wasn't an asset. She was considered attractive as well —she surmised with a complete and utter lack of vanity—and she'd only found it to be a *trap*.

"I wondered if you'd actually venture into the abyss, luv," he said idly, tugging a kerchief from his back pocket and across his sweaty brow.

He had a streak of graphite on his left cheek, and his hands were a further mess. Additionally, he'd made no effort to contain the twisted collar of his shirt. The top two bone buttons were undone, and the flash of olive skin drew her gaze when she wished it wouldn't. No coat, no waistcoat. He was unprepared for visitors. However, if she were being fair, she'd given him no notice he was to have one.

"Those feral phaeton rides through Hyde Park I read about in the *Gazette* must be true. They say you're a daredevil at heart, Templeton, a feminine trait the *ton* despises, am I right? Gossip that I'd lay odds you don't welcome any more than that charming nickname your poisonous brethren saddled you with." He tucked the length of stained cloth in his waistband to crudely dangle, drawing her eye to his trim waist. "They can't understand anyone of means who doesn't simply sit back and enjoy it."

"I'm, well…" Hildy fumbled, then wished she'd waited another moment to gather her thoughts. "I'm here on business. As you know. Or guessed."

His gaze dropped to the folio in her hand, his lips quirking sourly. "My sordid past is bundled up in that tidy file, I'm guessing."

No, actually, she wanted to admit but thankfully didn't. *I've gone into this all wrong.*

She ran through the facts detailed on the sheet in her wafer-thin folio that were not facts at all. Royal Navy hero of some sort, a conflict in India he didn't discuss publicly. Powerful friends in the East India Company, hence his move into trade upon his return to England. Ruthless, having built his empire one brick at a time. Father rumored to be titled, mother of Romani stock, at least a smidgen, which was all it took to be completely ostracized.

Insanely handsome had never factored into her research.

And she'd assumed this would be an uncomplicated

assignment.

"Tobias Streeter," he murmured, halting before her. Almost as tall as his brutish gatekeeper, Hildy kept her head tilted to capture his gaze. Which she was going to capture. And *hold.* Hazy light from a careless sun washed over him from windows set at all angles, allowing her to peruse at her leisure.

She didn't fool herself; it was an opportunity he *allowed.*

Skin the color of lightly brewed tea. Eyes the shade of a juicy green apple you shined against your sleeve and then couldn't help but take a quick bite of—the glow from the sconce turning them a deep emerald while she stared. Highlighted by a set of thick lashes any woman would be jealous of. Jaw hard, lips full, breath scented with mint and tea. Not brandy or scotch, another misstep had she presumed it.

When, of course, she'd presumed it.

As he patiently accepted her appraisal, his hand rose, and his index finger, just the calloused tip, trailed her cheek to tuck a stray strand behind her ear.

The hands of a man who worked with them.

Played with them.

She shivered, a shallow exhalation she couldn't contain rushing forth in a steamy puff. Parts of the ground story were open from quay to yard for transit handling, and glacial gusts were whistling through like a train on tracks.

"Alton," he instructed without glancing away from her, though he dropped his hand to his side. "Close the doors at the back, will you? And bring tea to my office."

"Tea," Alton echoed. "*Tea?*"

Streeter's breath fanned her face, warming her to her toes. "Isn't that what ladies drink over business dealings? If ladies even *do* business. Perhaps it's what they drink over spirited discussions about watercolors or their latest gown."

She gripped the folio until her knuckles ached, feeling like a ball of yarn being tossed between two cats. "Make no special accommodations. I'll have whatever it is you guzzle during business dealings, Mr. Streeter."

He laughed, then caught himself with the slightest downward tilt of his lips. She'd surprised them both somehow. It was the first chess move she'd won in this match. "We guzzle malt whiskey then," he murmured and turned, seeming to expect her to follow.

She recorded details as she shadowed him across the vast space crowded with shipping crates and assorted stacks of rope and tools, to a small room at the back overlooking the pier. His shirt was untucked on one side, the kerchief he'd wiped his face with slapping his thigh. His clothing was finely made but not skillfully enough to hide a muscular build most men used built-in padding to establish. Dark hair, *no*, more than dark. Black as tar, curling over his rumpled shirt collar and around his ears. So pitch dark, she imagined she could see cobalt streaks in it, like a flame gone mad.

Hair that called a woman's fingers to tangle in it, no matter the woman.

The gods had allotted this conceited beast an inequitable share of beauty, that was certain. And for the first time in her *life*, Hildy was caught up in an attraction.

His office was another unsurprising surprise.

A roaring fire in the hearth chasing away the chill. A Carlton House desk flanked by two armchairs roomy enough to fit Streeter or his man of business, Alton. A Hepplewhite desk, or a passable imitation. A colorful Aubusson covering the floor, nothing threadbare and sold because it had lost its value. Her heart skipped as she stepped inside the space, confirmation that she'd indeed misjudged. Shelf upon shelf of leather-bound books bracketed the walls. Walking to a row, she checked the spines with a searching review. Cracked but good, each and every one of them. Architecture, commerce, mathematics, chemistry. Nothing entertaining, nothing playful. The library of a man with a mind.

While Streeter moved to a sideboard that had likely come from the king's castoffs, and poured them a drink from a bottle whose label she didn't recognize, she circled the room, inspecting.

Holding both glasses in one hand, he situated himself not at his desk but on the edge of an overturned crate beside it, his long legs stretched before him. Sipping from his while holding hers, his steely gaze tracked her. Fortunately, she realized from the travel-weary Wellington he tapped lightly on the carpet, her examination of his private space was making him uneasy. With an aggrieved grunt, he yanked the kerchief from his waistband and tossed it needlessly to the floor.

Finally, she sighed in relief, a *weakness*. If he didn't like to be studied, he must have *something* to hide. She'd been hired, in part, to find out what.

"This isn't one of your frivolous races through the park." He leaned to place her glass on the corner of his desk. Hers to take, or not, when she passed. The only charitable thing he'd done was pour it for her. "Right now, I have two men guarding your traveling chariot parked outside, lest someone rob you blind. The thing is as yellow as a ripe banana, which catches the eye. They'll slice the velvet from the squabs and resell it two blocks over for fast profit. Your post-boy looked ready to expire when we got to him. Guessing he's never had to sit on his duff while waiting for his mistress to complete business in the East End. A slightly larger *man* might better fit the bill next time."

Post-boys were all she could afford.

Hildy released the satin chin strap and slid her bonnet from her head. Her coiffure, unsteady on a good day as her maid's vision was dreadful, collapsed with the removal, and a wave of hair just a shade darker than the sun fell past her shoulders. Streeter blinked, his fingers tightening around his glass. She noticed the insignificant gesture while wondering if the fevered awareness filling the air was only in *her* mind.

Halting by his desk, she reached for her drink with a nod in his direction. The scent of soap and spice drifted to her, his unique mix. "This warehouse, it's quite unusual. Magnificent, actually. I've never seen the like."

"I'll be sure to tell the architect the daughter of an earl approves." His gaze cool, giving away absolutely nothing, he dug a bamboo toothpick from his trouser pocket and jammed it between his teeth, working it from side to side between a pair of very firm lips. At her raised brow, he shrugged. "Stopped smoking. It's enough to breathe London's coal-laden air without asking for more trouble."

Hildy dropped the folio, which held little of value aside from her employment contract with the Earl of Hastings, in the armchair and lifted the glass to her lips. The whiskey was smooth, smoky—*good*. "This is excellent," she mused, licking her lips and watching Streeter's hand again tense around his tumbler.

"Thank you. It's my own formula," he said after a charged silence, a dent appearing next to his mouth. Not so much a dimple. Two of which she had herself, a feature people had commented on her entire life.

His was more of an elevated smirk.

"Yours?" Continuing her journey around the room, Hildy paused by a framed blueprint of this warehouse. Beside it was another detailed sketch, a building she didn't recognize. Architectural schematics drawn by someone very talented. She couldn't miss the initials, *TS*, in the lower right corner.

Frowning, she tilted her glass, staring into it as if the amber liquor would provide answers to an increasingly enigmatic puzzle. Aside from disappointing her family and society, she'd never done anything remarkable. *Been* anything remarkable.

When faced with remarkability, she wasn't sure she trusted it.

Streeter stacked his boots one atop the other, the crate creaking beneath him. "A business venture, a distillery going south financially that I found myself uncommonly intrigued by, once I handed over an astounding amount of blunt to keep it afloat *and* demanded I be invited into the process. Usually, I invest, then step away if the enterprise is well-managed, which it often isn't, but this…" Bringing the glass to his lips, he drank around the toothpick. Quite a feat. She couldn't look away from the show of masculine bravado if she'd been ordered to at the end of a pistol. "It's straightforward chemistry, the brewing of malt. But, lud, what a challenge, seeking perfection."

Finessing his glass into an empty spot next to him on the crate, he wiggled the toothpick from his lips and pointed it at her. A crude signal that he was ready to begin negotiations. "Isn't seeking perfection your business too, luv? The *ideal* bloke, without shortcomings. I've yet to see such a man, but the Mad Matchmaker is fabled to work miracles, so maybe there's a chance for me."

Seating herself in the chair absent her paperwork, Hildy set her glass on the desk and worked her gloves free, one deliberate finger at a time. If he believed he could chase her away with his bullying attitude, he hadn't done suitable research into his opponent's background. Last year, the Duchess Society had completed an assignment, confidential in nature but rumored nonetheless, for the royal family. Madness, power, fantastic wealth, love gained, love lost. This handsome scoundrel and his trifling reach for society's acceptance, she could handle.

Although she realized she was silently reminding herself of the fact, not stating it outright.

"Nothing to do with perfection and rarely anything to do with love, Mr. Streeter. The betrothals I support are, like the marriage you're proposing with Lady Matilda Delacour-Baynham, a business agreement. Unless I'm mistaken from the discussions I've had with her and her father, the Earl of Hastings."

He twirled the toothpick between his fingers like a magician. "You have it dead on. Holy hell, I'm not looking for love. Don't fill the chit's head with that rubbish. The words mean nothing to me.

They never have. Society only sells the idea to make the necessity of unions such as these more acceptable."

Well, *that* sounded personal. "Lady Matilda—"

"Mattie wants freedom. If you know her, she's told you what she's interested in. The only thing. Medicine." He laughed and sent the toothpick spinning. "An earl's daughter, can you conjure it? When no female can be a physician and certainly not a legitimate lady. To use one of your brethren's expressions, it's beyond the pale."

He winked at her, *winked*, and she was reasonably certain he didn't mean it playfully.

"I have funds, more than she can spend in a lifetime. More than I can. She wants to use a trifling bit to rescue her father, a man currently drowning, and I do mean drowning, in debt? Fine. Finance her hobby of practicing medicine? Also fine. Or her *dream*, if you're the visionary sort. Let her safely prowl these corridors and others on the rookery trail, delivering babes, bandaging wounds, swabbing fevered brows. They have no one else, the desperate souls I live amongst. She'll be an angel in their midst. And me, the one controlling the deliverance. Deliverance for *her* from your upmarket bunch. Who, other than finding ways to creatively lose capital, do nothing but sit around on their arses making up nicknames for those who *prosper*."

"What's in it for you?" Hildy whispered, not sure she knew. Was Tobias Streeter, rookery bandit, shipping titan, this eager to marry into a crowd that indeed sat on their toffs all day dreaming up pointless monikers? When she'd been trying to escape them her entire *life*?

He jabbed the toothpick in her direction, his smile positively savage. "Don't worry about what I need. I don't make deals where I don't profit, luv."

A caged tiger set loose on society. That's what he was. Half of London was secretly fawning over him while refusing him admittance to their sacred drawing rooms.

Not so fussy about admittance to their beds, she'd bet.

He slipped the toothpick home between his stubbornly compressed lips. "Templeton, you of all people should understand her predicament, being somewhat peculiar yourself. Boxed in by society's expectations, unless I'm missing my guess, which I usually don't. I understand, do you see? It's why the girl trusts me. Why, maybe, I trust *her*.

"I know what it's like to be found lacking for elements beyond your control. Where you were born, the color of your skin. Being delivered on the wrong side of some addled viscount's blanket. Think nothing of intelligence or courage, wit or ingenuity, *talent*, only the blue blood, or lack of it, running beneath that no one sees unless you slice them open."

Hildy smoothed her hand down her bodice and laid her gloves in a neat tangle on her knee, Streeter chasing every move with his intense, sea-green gaze. That blasted blue blood he spoke of kept her tangled in a web, day in and day out. He didn't need to enlighten her. Resignedly, she nodded to the folio lying like a spent weapon between them.

"Let's discuss specifics, shall we? Hastings wants you to court his daughter properly. Even if Lady... um, Mattie doesn't require it, *he* does. Flowers, gifts, trinkets. Courtship rituals. The servants gossip, and everyone in London then knows what's what, so this is an essential, seemingly trivial part of the process. I'll assist with the selection. He'd also like certain businesses you're involved with downplayed, so to speak. The unsavory enterprises. At least until the first babe is born. Rogue King of Limehouse Basin isn't exactly what he desired for his darling girl. But you, obviously, got to her first."

"At least I'm not an ivory-turner," he whispered beneath his breath.

She tilted her head in confusion.

"Her father cheats at dice, my naïve hoyden. I do many cursed things, but cheating is not one. Every gaming hell in town is after him." Streeter growled and, snatching up his glass, polished off the contents. Lord, she wished he'd button his collar. The view was becoming a distraction. "There's more to this agreement. I can see from the brutal twist of those comely lips of yours. More edges to be smoothed away like sandpaper to rough timber. Go on, spit it out. I can take a ruthless assessment."

Hildy controlled, through diligence born of her own beatdowns, the urge to raise her hand to cover her lips. *Comely* ones that had begun to sting pleasantly at his backhanded compliment. "Aside from your agreement that my solicitors—in addition to yours and the earl's—will review all contracts to ensure fairness for both parties, there is the matter of Miss Henson."

He whispered a curse against crystal and was unapologetic when his narrowed gaze met hers. He lowered his glass until it rested on his flat belly. "So, I'm to play the holy man until the ceremony?" Then he muttered something she didn't catch. Or didn't want to. *For a wife who prefers women.*

Hildy made a mental note to investigate that disastrous possibility, although it made no difference. Lady Matilda—Mattie—had to get married to someone. A *male* someone. Why not this beautiful devil who seemed to actually *like* her? Heavens, Hildy thought in despair. The Duchess Society couldn't weather the storm should a scandal of that magnitude come to light. It was illegal, which was absurd, of course, but that was the case. There were whisperings of such goings-on, relationships on the sly.

Rumors with the power to destroy one's *life*.

It was decided at that moment, with dust motes swirling through fading wintry sunlight, in a startlingly elegant office in the middle of a slum. This marriage, between a lady who wanted to be a doctor but couldn't and a tenacious blackguard who wanted high society tucked neatly in his pocket, had to happen. Or Hildy and her enterprise to save the women of London from gross matrimonial injustice was *finished*.

Too, she would go belly up without funds coming in to pay the bills—and coming in *soon*.

Streeter rocked forward, his Wellingtons dusting the floor, upsetting the shipping crate until she feared it would collapse beneath him. "I return the question because it's a valuable one. Besides a hefty fee that Hastings can't afford and will eventually derive from other sources, namely the source sharing this stale malt air with you, what's in it for you? Dealing with me isn't going to be easy. Ask my partners, should you be able to locate them. Mattie isn't much better from what I know of her. Her spirit is part of the reason I believed she'd be the right woman for the job."

Hildy chewed on her bottom lip, an abominable habit, then glanced up to find Streeter's gaze had gone vacant around the edges. The way a man's does when he's *thinking* about things. She wasn't, saints above, imagining the thread of attraction strung between them like ship's netting. He felt it, too. "I'll be candid."

"Please do," he whispered, bringing himself back from his musing, his cheeks slightly tinged. His breathing maybe, *maybe*, churning faster.

"When I arrived, I would've said I was doing it to secure future business with the Earl of Hastings. He has five daughters, as you know, and no wife to guide them. A line of inept governesses, another quitting every week it seems. My proposal?

"I guide him to appropriate men for the remaining four since Mattie has you on the hook. *Decent* men my people have investigated thoroughly. Then assist with the negotiations, so his daughters are protected, pay my coal bill, and we're both happy." Hildy ran her finger over a nap in the chair's velvet, her gaze dropping to record her progress. "Frankly, I need the money as I wasn't left a large inheritance, more a burden. An ever-maturing residence and staff and no funds allocated for preservation.

"And I'm not planning to marry myself, so survival falls directly to me. Likewise, I do this to benefit the young women I work with, if you must know, not simply as a business venture. You have no idea how lacking they are simply from being isolated from any discussions outside the appropriate tea to serve. They're forced to sign contracts they can't even begin to understand—*lifelong*, binding contracts—with no assistance."

The toothpick bounced in Streeter's mouth as he bit down on it. "What's changed?"

Digging her fingertips into the chair's cushion, she decided to tell him. "I'm *bored* with earls and viscounts in fretful need of an heir to carry on a line that should cease production. In need of capital to salvage a crumbling empire. A rumored Romani bastard who's hiding what he really wants, and I'm the person hired to find out what?" She snapped her fingers, a weight lifting as she spoke the truth. "Now, there's a challenge."

For a breathless second, Streeter's face erased of expression. Like a fist swept across a mirror's vapor. She'd stunned him—and her pulse soared. Foolishly, categorically. Then a broad smile, a *sincere* smile, sent the dent in his cheek pinging. His teeth flashed in wonderfully startling contrast to his olive skin. "Well, damn, I can be surprised." He saluted her with the glass he'd picked up only to find it empty. "A worthy opponent steps out of the mist."

"I'm not an opponent," she murmured, knowing she was.

With a sigh of regret, perhaps because she'd gone back to fibbing, he braced his hand on his thigh and rose to his feet. She watched him cross the room because she couldn't help herself. Tall, broad yet lean, an awe-inspiring physique even in mussed clothing. He moved with an innate grace even a duke wouldn't necessarily have possessed. Natural and unassuming. The stuff one was born with—or without. Elegance that simply was.

He stopped before another of the schematic drawings, an imposing brick structure laid out with mathematical precision she suspected existed only in the sketch. "What if I say no to working with you? Refuse your kind service. Toss it back to

Hastings like a flaming ember, pitting his desperation against my ambition."

Hildy understood after a moment's panic that this was part of the negotiation. That the correct response, or non-response, was vital. Retrieving her glass, she took a generous pull, smooth liquor chasing away the chill. "Is it any different than working with your"—she gestured over her shoulder to the warehouse—"bountiful trading partners? We'll be in business together. End of story."

He paused, studying her in a way few men had dared to even while telling her how beautiful she was. Men she'd never wanted to undress her with their eyes, as the saying went. A phrase that until this second had held no meaning.

A peculiar tension, the awareness from earlier, roared between them as if Alton had reopened the doors and let the Thames rush in. As if Tobias Streeter had laid his hands on her. An experience she had no familiarity with which to visualize.

"End of story," he murmured joylessly and turned back to his sketch.

She deposited her folio on his desk, the thump ringing through the room. Outside, a dockworker's shout and the rub and bump of a ship sliding into harbor pierced the hush. He was equally damaged, she could see. And very good at hiding it. They were alike in this regard, a mysterious element only another wounded animal would recognize.

Making the call on instinct alone, Hildy nonetheless made it.

Tobias Streeter wasn't a fiend. He wasn't an abuser like her father.

He was just a man.

A man she was willing to polish until he shone like the crown jewels. "There will be events. Part of your engagement and intro-duction to the *ton*, as it were. You'll likely need some instruction."

He tapped the sketch three times before shifting to lean his shoulder against the wall in a negligent slump she no longer counted as factual. "I clean up well. Never fear," he said, his voice laced with scorn. Who it was directed at, she wasn't sure. "I'll review the contract in that tasteful folio of yours this evening, then we'll discuss the details tomorrow afternoon. I'll send a carriage with a coachman ready to protect you should the need arise, not those lads just out of the schoolroom you have manning your conveyance."

Glancing to a clock on the mantel that had been cautiously ticking off time, his smile thinned, frigid enough to freeze water. "I'm sorry to rush you out, but I have a meeting in ten minutes that will, if successful, net me close to a thousand pounds. My men will escort you home. Your chariot can follow along for fun." His jaw tensed when she started to argue, and he pushed off the wall with a growl. "Not on my watch, Templeton. Not in my township. Don't even *begin*."

However, stubborn chit that she was, she did begin, opening her mouth to tell him who was managing this campaign to show London how bloody wonderful a husband he would be.

"Tea and some of them lemony biscuits from the baker on the corner, coming right up," Alton proclaimed, stumbling into the room, a silver teapot she wondered where in heaven's name he'd located clutched in a meaty fist and two mismatched china cups balanced in the other. Halting, he took one look at his employer's thunderous expression, slapped the cups on the first available surface, and hustled Hildy from the office.

The teapot was still in his hand as Streeter's coach rolled down the congested lane with her an unwilling captive inside. She suppressed a clumsy laugh to see a coat of arms, painted over but visible, on the carriage's door.

Another aristocrat who'd lost his fortune to the Rogue King.

Hildy collapsed against the plush squabs of the finest transport she'd ever ridden in, realizing she hadn't asked Tobias Streeter how he planned to profit from a marriage he didn't want.

ABOUT TRACY SUMNER

Tracy's story telling career began when she picked up a copy of LaVyrle Spencer's Vows on a college beach trip. A journalism degree and a thousand romance novels later, she decided to try her hand at writing a southern version of the perfect love story. With a great deal of luck and more than a bit of perseverance, she sold her first novel to Kensington Publishing.

When not writing sensual stories featuring complex characters and lush settings, Tracy can be found reading romance, snowboarding, watching college football and figuring out how she can get to 100 countries before she kicks. She lives in the south, but after spending a few years in NYC, considers herself a New Yorker at heart.

Tracy has been awarded the National Reader's Choice, the Write Touch and the Beacon—with finalist nominations in the HOLT Medallion, Heart of Romance, Rising Stars and Reader's Choice. Her books have been translated into German, Dutch, Portuguese and Spanish. She loves hearing from readers about why she tends to pit her hero and heroine against each other from the very first page or that great romance she simply must order in five seconds on her Kindle.

Connect with Tracy:

www.tracy-sumner.com

facebook.com/Tracysumnerauthor

twitter.com/sumnertrac

instagram.com/tracysumnerromance

bookbub.com/profile/tracy-sumner

amazon.com/Tracy-Sumner/e/B000APFV3G

pinterest.com/tracysumnerromance

Made in the USA
Las Vegas, NV
05 December 2023

82121197R00059